THE WILDLIFE DIVAS
ADVENTURE TEAM

THE WILDLIFE DIVAS ADVENTURE TEAM

Saving the Endangered Mountain Gorilla

Lisa M Randolph

Illustrations by Sofía Ruzo

NEW DEGREE PRESS

THE WILDLIFE DIVAS ADVENTURE TEAM

Saving the Endangered Mountain Gorilla

Illustrations by Sofía Ruzo

ISBN

978-1-63730-711-3   *Paperback*

978-1-63730-849-3   *Kindle Ebook*

979-8-88504-004-4   *Digital Ebook*

This book is dedicated to all

the GASA Girls of Sunnydale

&

My Littlest Wildlife Diva,

Scarlett Baran

FICTITIOUS CHARACTER DISCLAIMER

CONTENTS

———

CHAPTER 1
RAVENSWING ACADEMY

—

Lightening rarely strikes in San Francisco, but tonight the city was surprised by a late spring storm. The wind blew so hard, the rain fell sideways. The doorbell rang, followed by several rapid impatient knocks. The headmistress of the Ravenswing Academy for Girls viewed the security camera and rushed to the front door. Unconsciously, she smoothed back her neat stylishly cut, dark brown hair, which was never out of place. She swung open one side of the heavy wooden double doors. Lightning flashed behind the woman and small child standing in the doorway, illuminating them. She hurried them inside and out of the rain.

She had been waiting for their arrival. An earlier phone call that day explained the situation. It was an urgent placement. A nine-year-old girl needed immediate housing. They'd tried placing her in several different homes with no success. Luckily, there was one unoccupied bed left at Ravenswing.

The social worker and the headmistress spoke quietly as the little girl looked around the room. Occasionally they would look over at the child, who stood in one place, fidgeting.

Her hair, parted down the middle and secured with two rubber bands, looked like mouse ears. It wasn't the style that was odd, but the color. In fact, everything about her was the same hue: a fiery, reddish-brown. Her hair, skin, and even her lips were a pinkish red, and lastly her eyes were the color of honey.

The child noticed a fire blazing brightly. As quietly as a mouse, she took small, unsure steps until she stood in front of the fireplace. Mesmerized by the flames, the girl stood staring blankly, her eyes void of emotion. Fire. Fire was why she was here now. Fire stole all her dolls and books. Fire stole every stitch of clothing except the ones she wore. Fire made her an orphan. Fire.

Startled, the girl swung around quickly. She hadn't noticed the person on the sofa behind her. Seventeen-year-old Ebony lay stretched out on the couch. Her eyes closed, headphones covering her ears, listening to her new favorite Drake song. She snapped her fingers and sang softly, wagging her feet back and forth to a beat only she could hear.

Ebony opened her eyes to find a pair of honey-brown eyes staring directly into hers. She turned off the music on her phone and slid the headphones off.

"Hey," she waved. "Where did you come from?" She looked over her shoulder finding Miss Cherie escorting the social worker out the front door.

"You're the new girl, huh?" The girl did not respond but only stared.

"Do you need any help? Here, let me take this for you." Ebony tried to take the item she clutched tightly to her chest. The little girl's grip tightened, pulling back with force.

"All right, calm down already," Ebony said, annoyed. She was known for her short temperedness. In a sudden movement, she jumped up from the sofa and grabbed the item from the child's arms and laughed. "Ha ha!"

Shock was the first emotion to register on the girl's face. And if it were possible, her face turned redder than normal as she let out a loud cry that sounded more like an animal's growl, growing shrill and loud.

"Like, chill out already!" Ebony covered an ear with one hand while holding the broken toy in the air just out of the little girl's reach.

"Calm down and be quiet! You need an off switch?"

"Give it back!" The girl screeched. Angry tears spilled down her cheeks. She jumped up and down several times, grabbing at her prized possession held just out of reach.

The other girls, working on their science project, stopped mid-experiment and watched the drama unfold.

The girl looked like an angry bull seeing a red flag. She took a few steps back, lowered her head, and ran full speed. Ebony stumbled backward, making an "oof" sound as the girl rammed into her headfirst.

"Hey, you little twerp! Like, oh my god, are you serious?" Ebony wasn't hurt, but now she was definitely miffed! "I was only trying to help you with your belongings!" She rubbed her belly, which was starting to grow tender after being rammed.

The girl with the measuring cup filled with vinegar was so busy watching Ebony and the girl, she accidentally poured the vinegar into the funnel sitting in the mouth of the volcano.

Do you know what happens when you mix baking soda and vinegar together? The volcano exploded, a stream of colored foam came shooting out of the opening and nearly touching the ceiling before splattering all over the countertops and floors. What a mess!

Miss Cherie walked in at that precise moment to find the entire room in chaos. Foaming liquid was spouting everywhere, the little girl was ramming Ebony in the belly, Ebony was yelling, and the girl was crying and kicking.

"What in the world is going on here!" Miss Cherie's voice sounded loud and shrill above the hullabaloo. Each one of them froze at the sound of her voice. Both hands upon each hip, she assessed the situation. It was not good.

"You! Stop teasing her and give it back! Now!" she said, pointing a finger at Ebony. "And you three," she pivoted, pointing the same finger at Yalani, Valerie, and Kyloni, "clean up this mess!"

Ebony reluctantly gave back the child's toy. She rubbed her leg where the girl kicked her hard. And deservedly so, according to Miss Cherie. She took the child by the shoulders and guided her toward the hallway leading to the bedrooms.

"Come along, Storm, let's get you ready for bed and a good night's sleep. We have a big day ahead of us tomorrow. Let's see if we can introduce ourselves properly in the morning."

"Storm? Her name is Storm? How appropriate." Kyloni snort-laughed as she pushed up her eyeglasses hanging from the tip of her nose.

"What a stormy little *brat* is more like it!" Ebony glared as they walked past.

Storm, hearing Ebony's comment, turned, wrinkled her nose, and stuck out her tongue. She hugged the broken bug catcher tightly to her chest as Miss Cherie escorted her down the hallway.

"That old thing is dirty, nasty, and it's broken." Ebony called after her. She always had to get the last word in.

* * *

Every day of the week, except weekends, the alarm clocks went off at six o'clock in the morning. It gave everyone one hour to shower, brush their teeth, get dressed, and assemble at the kitchen table. At 7 a.m., breakfast was served. Today's menu was eggs, waffles with all the extras, soy yogurt, fruits, berries, and coconut water for the vegetarians.

After breakfast, it was time for the daily morning check-in meeting in front of the fireplace.

Normally, they would attend homeschooling after their meeting. Their advanced curriculum was taught by none other than Miss Cherie, who was currently earning her doctorate degree in education. Although the girls were technically considered orphans, they were each specially chosen to live here at Ravenswing Academy for their extraordinary talents and marked intelligence.

Today was different. It was their annual camping trip. Three days and two nights of sleeping outdoors under the stars. Hopefully they would not have the same problem as last year's trip: dealing with a bear strolling into their camp. That night no one slept as they huddled together in fear.

Miss Cherie began the meeting. She stood before the group as they sat on the sofa directly in front of the fireplace where the fire crackled, warming the chilly morning air.

"Before we leave this morning, we need to discuss what happened last night. There will be no bullying here at Ravenswing," she said sternly. "It will not be tolerated. I don't want to ever see what happened last night again." She looked at Ebony, who lowered her head and looked away.

"We only have each other. We must respect each other. And when we see someone being mistreated, we must speak up. Each one of you can understand this." She finished her speech. "Let's introduce ourselves to our newest member." There were five in all. "We'll start from the oldest to the youngest. Ebony, you go first."

Ebony flipped her long tresses of brightly colored hair. This week she'd chosen red and gold. You could hardly live in San Francisco and not see these colors; it was the color of the city's famous football team, the Forty-Niners. Her long nails were painted to match.

"Hey, I'm Ebony. I'm seventeen years old. I'm an artist and an Instagram influencer. I love taking selfies. I love fashion. And I am a very fun, kind person ..."

The last statement was met with a cough and the rolling of eyes. She could be called anything but kind and fun. If you didn't do what she wanted, you'd find yourself at her mercy.

"What?" she sneered. "I am fun!"

"Is there anything else you'd like to say?" Miss Cherie asked, ignoring her attitude. "Maybe an apology?"

"Oh yeah, that." She waved a dismissive hand, refusing to make eye contact with Storm. She refused to say her name. "I'm sorry about last night. It wasn't my fault. Why? Because I was just trying to help, and you spazzed out. You know that thing's broken, right? You should throw it in the trash."

Cherie stared at her with a stern look.

"That's enough, Ebony," she warned. She turned to Storm and asked, "Storm, do you accept Ebony's apology? If not, we'll keep discussing this until we get it resolved."

She nodded her head, up and down, signaling a "yes." Apology accepted.

"Are you sure?" Another nod. When Miss Cherie turned her back, Storm once again stuck out her tongue at Ebony.

"Okay, Kyloni, your turn," she continued.

"Yes, hello, my name is Kyloni." Her glasses slid down her nose. She pushed them back up with her index finger. "I've survived a total of fifteen earth orbits of 365.25 days around the sun." She snorted as she laughed at her own joke. Only Storm laughed with her. Everyone else had heard this before and didn't find it humorous at all.

"I love science and one day I will be a famous scientist. I'm not quite sure in what field of study just yet. I start my first year of college next semester."

"College?" Storm interrupted, observing how young she looked. "I thought you were like twelve years old."

It didn't help that she wore braided hair in two ponytails, oversized jeans with tattered bottoms that dragged the floor, old, cheap tennis shoes, and a t-shirt with Albert Einstein sticking out his tongue.

"It's true. I am what one would perceive as petite. I'll have you know that although I am small in stature and often mistaken for being much younger than I am, I have an exceptional prefrontal cortex and left temporal lobe, protected by my superbly formed cerebral cranium."

Ebony interrupted her. "Please don't start with the prefrontal mumbo jumbo again. I don't want to hear about it."

Kyloni continued, paying no attention to Ebony. "I've earned a 5.0 grade point average, which is why I'm starting college three years ahead of schedule." She sat down, quite pleased with herself and her accomplishments.

"Valerie," Miss Cherie coaxed. "It's your turn." She held her breath.

Thirteen-year-old Valerie looked down at her shoes, her voice barely above a whisper.

"My name is ... My name is Valerie, and I—I, I'm..." She stammered then stopped talking. She refused to say another word, her face growing a scarlet red. She swallowed the rising lump in her throat.

Miss Cherie comforted her. "It's okay, Valerie. No pressure. I want you to talk when you're ready. Okay?" Valerie nodded, embarrassed. Kyloni squeezed her shoulder. Their friendship had grown since her arrival, and she was the only person Valerie felt comfortable talking to.

Miss Cherie turned to Yalani. "Your turn."

Yalani was bright and bubbly. She wore her hair in a neatly brushed up-do with a single ponytail with a streak of pink and front bangs that she constantly pushed aside to keep hair out of her eyes.

"I'm Yalani. I'm eleven years old. I like to skateboard."

Ebony scoffed. "You've never even ridden your stupid skateboard even once. She's scared …"

"That's enough Ebony," Miss Cherie chided. "She will do it when she's good and ready. Now mind your business."

Yalani was dressed in her favorite skateboard outfit: a white t-shirt with an image of glittery sunglasses on the front, a pair of pink leggings, and, of all things, a tutu made with several layers of itchy pink tulle. She also had white, high-top tennis shoes. She had painted them with pink glitter hearts. In her hands she held, of course, a pink skateboard, which she named "Itzy Gurl" after her favorite K-pop girl band. She said as much when she introduced the skateboard to Storm like it was a real person.

"One day," she added, "I am going to be a skateboard champion."

Cherie turned to the youngest member of the group. "And last but not least, our new addition, Storm."

Storm suddenly felt shy with all the attention on her. She clutched her broken bug catcher tighter to her chest.

"Just say your name and how old you are. Don't be shy." Cherie encouraged her.

"Hi, my name is Storm and I'm nine years old. I don't like people touching my stuff." She sniffled and wiped her nose with the back of her long-sleeved shirt. She eyed Ebony, making her grimace in disgust. "Oh. And thank you Miss Cherie for my new clothes and new shoes. Um, and my new toothbrush. I like them very much."

She hugged the new youngest member, touched by her gratitude. "You're most welcome, Storm. And welcome to Ravenswing Academy; we're happy to have you. Now let's get the van packed! Ebony, you're in charge. Make sure you get an extra sleeping bag for Storm and extra blankets too. Let's get going, ladies." She clapped her hands, "Move it, time's a-wasting!" They rushed to get the van loaded, working as a team.

∗ ∗ ∗

They piled into the van, fastened their seat belts, and off they drove down the streets of their neighborhood. The buildings were old and neglected for many years. Some sat empty, abandoned, and boarded up, while others looked as if a fresh coat of paint would make it brand new. The truth was the city was going to tear down all the rows of crumbling townhomes and build new ones.

One apartment in particular Storm paid close attention to as they passed by. Yellow caution tape crisscrossed the front door and the upstairs windows were charred black where fire ravaged its insides. She turned away quickly, staring straight ahead without blinking, nervously clutching her broken bug catcher so tightly, her fingertips lost their color. Ebony followed her gaze, the only one to notice her reaction.

They arrived at the campgrounds after a shorter than usual ride. Half Moon Bay State Park, the sign read. The previous year they'd driven to Lake Tahoe, which was nearly a two-hour drive. That was where the bear walked through their campsite looking for food.

Storm couldn't contain her excitement. "We're camping at the beach?" Her voice shrill and high-pitched as she pressed her face against the van's window for a better look.

"Like, oh my god, can you calm down already. It's just a beach!" an annoyed Ebony protested. "And, uh, hello. You're standing on my shoe."

Storm quickly removed her foot from Ebony's hiking boot. She'd already learned to stay clear of her from last night's confrontation.

"I'm sorry for stepping on your shoe. It's just that I've never been to the beach before," she explained.

"Well, just be careful and watch your step." She swiped invisible dirt from her shoe. "I get you're excited." She was trying to be nicer. She had seen the look on Storm's face when they passed the burned-out home and figured it had something to do with her. It was probably the reason behind why she arrived last night in the middle of a storm.

"But before you can go down to the beach, you'll have to do your part, help unload the van and set up camp. You can help me put up the tent. Okay?"

"Okay." Storm replied in agreement. She almost smiled.

They set up a single tent that easily fit all six of them, their sleeping bags, and other belongings. The door faced the hanging cliffs overlooking the beach. That way when they woke in the morning, they would see the great Pacific Ocean and have the perfect view to catch beautiful sunsets at night. And if they were lucky, they could catch sight of whales and dolphins migrating from Mexico to Alaska in their yearly trip.

With their chores completed, they headed down the cliffs to the beach to collect items on their scavenger list. They searched for three different types of seashells, something blue, something triangle shaped, and more. They all laughed at one thing on the list: to find something stinky.

Along the beach they ran, laughing and chasing one another with pieces of seaweed and other "stinky" things when they spotted something in the distance. Cautiously they approached, thinking it was already dead. Valerie poked it with a piece of driftwood. They jumped back in surprise when the injured bird squawked noisily in protest at being disturbed. It was tangled in fishing line, a hook lodged in its mouth.

Ebony took charge, her voice serious and urgent.

"Run. Go get help! Go!"

What they didn't know, could never have guessed in a thousand years, was how their rescue attempt was about to make a colossal change in their lives.

CHAPTER 2

G-G-GORILLAS!

———

Several weeks later, the computer alert broke the silence. Miss Cherie sat at her computer desk, leaning back in alarmed surprise. A notification flashed across the screen of her laptop. Now she leaned forward for a better look. Peering closely, her lips moved rapidly as she read the first few lines of the email. Could it be true?

This is it! The email the girls had waited all summer to receive. They had kept up with their duties, chores, new lessons, and homeschool assignments. Miss Cherie monitored daily waiting in anticipation for this very email to arrive. She yelled at the top of her lungs,

"Girls, it's here! We have Diva Mail."

Her shout of nervous excitement was loud enough to be heard in every room of the group home. One by one, they rushed into the home office. Gathering around, they crowded Miss Cherie, their voices filled with excitement, all talking at once. It was unbelievable. The time had finally come. Their first assignment!

"I wonder where we're going," Valerie said in a voice barely above a whisper.

After their last camping trip, she had begun to open up a little and was now more comfortable talking to everyone, but still spoke so softly it was difficult to hear her at times.

"Remember we were told during orientation we could end up anywhere in the world."

"Me too, I can't wait to hear our first assignment. I wonder if we'll be asked to save another seagull," Kyloni said, remembering what a great time they'd had camping out at Half Moon Bay.

Yalani cringed, the memory causing her great anxiety.

"Oh no, oh my gosh, not another seagull! That bird nearly pecked my finger off!"

Storm giggled remembering the incident. The look of terror on Yalani's face when the seagull "pecked" her finger was funny. It was more like a chomp; the bird bit down and refused to let go. They had to pry her finger out of the bird's mouth with Yalani nearly fainting during the uproar.

"Shh, quiet you guys," Ebony chimed in with her usual impatience, "Let's find out where Dr. Khambrel's sending us. Cherie, hurry up and read the email. I can't stand the suspense!"

Miss Cherie began by reading the title of the email. "Ahem," she cleared her throat and read aloud. "Poachers—"

Immediately they all began to talk at once, interrupting her.

"What did she say? Did she say roaches?" Storm questioned, wide-eyed and hopeful. She loved bugs and even knew the scientific name for cockroaches: *Periplaneta Americana.*

"No, I think she said 'poachers,' silly, not roaches," Yalani teased.

"Oh …" Storm was thoughtful for a moment, curiosity getting the better of her. "What's a poacher?" she asked.

"Shh! Zip it!" Ebony said, even more impatient than before if that were at all possible. "Let her finish and she'll tell you!" She held a single finger to her lips.

Miss Cherie continued, "What is a poacher? Well, it says here in the email that poachers are individuals who illegally hunt, kill, capture, and kidnap endangered animals."

She paused for a moment while the girls nodded, even if they did not understand completely.

"Ah …" they said in unison.

Miss Cherie kept reading.

"Your assignment, if the Wildlife Divas Adventure Team chooses to accept, will take you 16,093 kilometers away from San Francisco to the Bwindi Impenetrable Forest—"

Once again, they interrupted.

"Ba—who? What kinda forest?" Storm asked.

"No. She said, Ba—windy penny—pasta forest." Yalani guessed.

"Don't be ridiculous. Pasta? What kind of forest is made of pasta?" Ebony questioned.

"Did she say 16,093 kilometers? That's far! Where's the map?" Kyloni looked for a map.

"Kilometers? How many miles is that?" Storm asked.

"Let's Diva Google it!" Kyloni suggested.

Storm stood behind Cherie, scanning the computer screen. She read the email for herself. She ping-ponged from one foot to the other.

"Oh, oh, I know where we're going! I know where we're going! We're going to Africa! We're going to Africa! A-fri-ca! A-fri-ca!" she chanted excitedly, dancing around the room in circles.

They looked back and forth at each other, wide-eyed. Africa? Did she just say they were going to Africa?

Miss Cherie chuckled at the expression on their faces. She laughed and continued reading.

"You will arrive in the city of Kampala, in the East African country of Uganda, where you will hike into the rain forest to help stop *poachers* by finding and destroying traps and snares. In turn, this keeps them from kidnapping the babies of the critically endangered Mountain Gorilla."

Storm stopped dead in her tracks, mid-dance. Did she hear correctly? The other girls finally stopped talking and their eyes grew wide with the shocking news they'd just heard. Storm, although she was the youngest and smallest of the group, yelled so loud her voice echoed and the entire room shook.

"G-G-Gorillas!"

Behind them came a loud shriek of terror and then a muffled *thump*!

"*Storm!*" Ebony screeched, as they all covered their ringing ears with both hands.

"Oops, sorry, that was loud, huh?" Storm shrugged her shoulders with a half-embarrassed smile. "But—but she said we were going to find gorillas." She pointed a finger of blame at Miss Cherie.

"Hey! What was that sound?"

They immediately turned their attention to the sound of the *thump*. It was Yalani sprawled out on the floor. At the word *gorillas,* she'd let out a terrified scream and fainted.

Rushing to her side, the team went into action caring for their fallen Diva. Cherie sent Storm rushing for a cool wet towel. Valerie and Kyloni took turns fanning her face, gently calling her name, while Ebony decided a slap or two on the cheek was in order. She not-so-gently slapped one side of her face and then the other. This seemed to work as Yalani's eyes fluttered open.

"Yalani, are you okay?" Cherie asked. Storm handed her the wet towel and placed it on Yalani's forehead.

"Wha—what happened?" Yalani stammered, dazed and a little confused. "How'd I end up on the floor?"

Kyloni explained as she pushed her glasses up with an index finger.

"Most likely insufficient oxygenated blood flow to the cerebral cortex causing a disruption of neural activity to the brain, which resulted in a temporary loss of consciousness."

Yalani just stared. She didn't understand a word Kyloni had said.

"You fainted." Kyloni said matter-of-factly.

"I—I did?" Yalani uttered in disbelief.

"Yeah." Storm added, demonstrating. "I said 'gorillas,' and you said 'ah!' and

then you went 'oom, Pow' and landed like this." Storm fell onto the floor next to Yalani, her eyes closed, her tongue sticking out the side of her mouth.

"No, I didn't!" Yalani laughed, removing the cool cloth from her forehead. She was already beginning to feel better.

Valerie and Kyloni helped her to her feet.

"Oh my gosh, but seriously, I thought you said something about gorillas. Now that's a scary thought—gorillas." Nervously she turned to Cherie, clutching one side of her chest. "You almost gave me a heart attack."

It was then she noticed the serious look on her face and knew she wasn't kidding.

"Yes, Yalani." Miss Cherie explained, keeping her voice calm and rational. She was trying to avoid another fainting spell. "We are going to save Mountain Gorillas in Africa. We are going to hike into the rainforest and perhaps, if we complete our mission, we may come face to face with the gorillas. Or maybe we'll run into some awfully bad people while we're at it." Miss Cherie could see Yalani was still afraid.

"This is our job as wildlife ambassadors," Miss Cherie cautioned. "You can't be so afraid that you're paralyzed with fear from the smallest things. We have important work to do, saving these animals. Are you sure you can do this, Yalani? If not, we'll have to find another young lady to replace you."

Yalani closed her eyes and took a few deep breaths and calmed herself. She did not want to be replaced. From now on, she would try harder to be brave.

She opened her eyes and stood up straight. She felt a little braver. Yalani looked at Cherie and at each member of her team.

"I pinky swear. I promise I'm coming, and I'll do my best." She meant it. She made a fist and stuck out her pinky finger for each one of them to grab, sealing her promise.

"I'm glad to hear that." Cherie was satisfied with her answer. "Remember, Yalani, our entire team is here to support you. So, if you find yourself feeling afraid, we've got your back!" She gave Yalani a hug.

Hearing this helped soothe her; she smiled weakly and swallowed the lump of fear in her throat.

"Now! Let's get started with a little research about our assignment," Cherie said taking a seat at the computer desk again. "Before we get started, I don't want any interruptions this time. I'll answer any questions after I finish reading the email. Agreed?"

They all agreed.

* * *

Gathering as much information as possible, they sat down to plan their trip. Kyloni grabbed her iPad and typed into the Diva Google search field *"Uganda Bwindi Impenetrable Forest"* and hit enter. She found the website for the Ugandan Wildlife Authority. She browsed the homepage. After several clicks, she found what she was looking for.

"Bwindi Impenetrable National Park"
(B-win-di Im-pe-ne-tra-ble)

Kyloni pushed up her glasses with one finger and began to read.

"The Bwindi Impenetrable National Park lies in southwestern Uganda on the edge of the Rift

Valley. It's mist-covered hillside are blanketed by one of Uganda's oldest and most biologically diverse rainforests, which dates back over 25,000 years and contains almost 400 species of plants. More famously, this 'impenetrable forest' also protects an estimated 320 mountain gorillas: roughly half of the world's population."

She stopped reading to make an observation.

"'Roughly half of the world's population?' 320 gorillas. That's not very many. I understand why our assignment is so important."

A sense of urgency and the importance of their work suddenly struck a chord within her. These animals were on the verge of extinction.

"We must stop these poachers from kidnapping baby mountain gorillas. They are rapidly decreasing the population. Do you guys understand what this means? It means if we are not successful, there is a great possibility that these gorillas could disappear off the face of the earth. Like the dinosaurs, like—like the West African Black Rhinoceros. Disappear completely, as in *no more gorillas* in the rainforest. Complete annihilation! Extinction!"

Strong emotions powered her words. It was a sobering thought, the loss of an entire species.

Just as she finished her impassioned speech, Ebony's bedroom door flew open with a bang. No one had noticed that she'd slipped away to her bedroom. Now here she was without a clue of what they were talking about. She had not heard a word of Kyloni's impassioned plea.

Ebony's obsession was hair, nails, make-up, designer clothing, and social media. She walked into the room like a fashion model on a catwalk. There might as well have been a dozen paparazzi with their cameras flashing from all directions. She was like a superstar with her adoring fans shouting her name. A fashionista, a trend setter. She spent endless hours on social media posting make-up and fashion tips to her nearly hundred thousand followers.

She was quite popular.

One by one they turned to look at Ebony. She was looking kinda cute in the outfit she'd chosen. She wore a pink baseball cap with the word DIVA in rhinestones and a white blouse tied in front with a pink tank-top underneath. She also had a pair of brown khaki shorts rolled up and a pair of four-inch-high heels with a camouflage pattern. (They were going to a jungle, after all.) To the outfit she added jewelry, rings, bracelets, necklaces, and a pair of mirrored aviator sunglasses. Cute!

Ebony admired herself in the mirror, pushing a wayward curl of hair back in place.

"Like, oh my god. I look so adorable. I'm wearing this outfit on the first day of our gorilla thingy or whatever."

She had a strong California accent. Ebony posed, taking several selfies with her phone. She was just getting started. She would tweet and post at least a dozen photos on Instagram before too long.

They looked at her admiringly, all except Valerie who'd just finished reading about the type of clothing they should wear. And what Ebony had chosen would not be the proper clothing for hiking in a rainforest. She took in her appearance, smiled, and said nothing. Just shook her head from side to side.

"Oh my god! What?" Ebony turned in annoyance to face Valerie. She'd added an oversized designer travel bag to her ensemble.

"First of all," she spoke quietly, calmly, not liking confrontation, "I'd like to say I really love your outfit, Ebony, but …"

"But what?" Ebony was preparing for an argument.

"But," Valerie continued softly, "it says here that we need protective clothing."

"So, what does that have to do with me?" Ebony rudely interrupted, cutting her off. She was beginning to lose patience and this conversation was quickly becoming boring.

"Apparently, there are lots of disease-carrying insects. Bugs. Flying, biting, stinging bugs that love fresh meat to nibble on." Ebony's bare arms and legs were a bug's feast waiting to happen. "I mean it's entirely up to you; you don't have to take the recommended advice, but me personally. Me? I'll be wearing what's suggested by the experts: long sleeved shirts and pants, thick socks, and hiking boots to make sure my skin is covered. And this will help keep my feet warm and dry."

Knowing Ebony's hatred for anything that creeps or crawls, she added, "I don't want bugs hitchhiking a ride on me. Can you imagine bugs crawling up and down your arms and legs, or maybe a big fat spider taking a little ride in your hair? Nope, not me. I will be dressed properly. But wear what you wish. Your outfit is really cute."

Ebony shuddered, imagining bugs between her toes, biting and nibbling on her exposed skin. Or worse, a spider in her hair. Ebony rolled her eyes, abruptly turned on her heels, and stomped out of the room.

"So annoying!" she mumbled under her breath as she left. "And such a know-it-all!" Away she went to rethink her wardrobe.

Valerie added, "A raincoat and rain boots would probably be a good idea too." To that, Ebony angrily slammed her bedroom door shut.

"Drama queen." Storm expressed what they were thinking.

Cherie gave her a glance over the top of her glasses. "Be nice," she warned with a hint of a smile.

"Okay, okay, see?" Storm made an imaginary zipper across her lips and tossed away the imaginary key.

Cherie checked her watch, noting the time. "Well, ladies, we need to get going. There are several things we must complete today before we can leave for Africa. One of which includes shopping and for the correct type of clothing. She emphasized the word "*shopping*," saying it loud enough for Ebony to hear behind the closed bedroom door.

On cue she opened the door, just enough to peek out. "Like, okay, did I hear you say we're going shopping?" Ebony questioned, no longer angry at the thought of buying new clothes. Cherie now had her full and undivided attention.

"Yes, we're going shopping and taking care of a couple other important matters before we leave. Grab your things and let's go!" Cherie reached for the car keys.

"Good! Retail therapy." Ebony grabbed her purse and sunglasses, nearly to the front door.

"Last one to the car is a rotten egg!" Storm yelled playfully as she darted past Ebony.

"I'm riding shotgun!" Yalani shouted.

As she reached the door Cherie stopped and turned to look at them. Each offered something unique to the team. They fidgeted under her inspection, not sure what she wanted to say to them.

"I'm proud of each and every one of you. What we're doing has tremendous value. We are saving lives and it is a great responsibility." She was nearly moved to tears; she felt such pride. "And it's my honor and a privilege to embark on this adventure with you."

"Aw, we love you too, Cherie." Valerie whispered with a shy smile and hugged her. They were proud of her as well.

"C'mon, group hug." Valerie stretched out her arms to everyone as they gathered Cherie into a big, warm embrace.

They were the Wildlife Divas Adventure Team, and their first international adventure was about to begin.

.

CHAPTER 3

HOT SHOTS

Standing next to the nurses station, Miss Cherie stooped down to make eye contact with the salty-tempered nine-year-old standing in front of her. She'd expected Yalani to be trouble but was surprised by Storm's stubbornness.

"Storm, you must do this or you can't go. It's as simple as that." She threw both hands up in despair. She was getting vexed with the situation.

Storm continued to pout, arms folded tightly across her chest. The look on her face left no doubt, she was pretty upset about something.

"No," she replied, dead set against the idea.

Valerie tried coaxing her. She whispered, "Please Storm, the trip won't be the same without you. C'mon, would you like me to hold your hand?"

She answered again, this time she stomped her foot. "No. You can't make me!"

Ebony chimed in, her usual un-charming self. "Like, oh my god, stop being a brat, Brat!"

Storm glared at Ebony, wrinkled her nose, and stuck out her tongue.

Kyloni attempted to comfort her with an explanation. "You may experience a slight unpleasant sensation. It is merely special nerves that detect tissue damage transmitting information along the spinal cord to the brain. Here, watch. I'll go first."

Kyloni sat down, clearly unafraid, and she rolled up both sleeves. A nurse with two rather large needles administered the vaccines in one arm and then the other.

"Ouch," she said, and it was over. "You see Storm, just a tiny, microscopic pinch. No big deal. It feels like … like a mosquito bite. Did you know the word 'mosquito' means 'little fly' in the Spanish language?" Using an index finger, she pushed up her eyeglasses. For an instant, she looked like a bug-eyed mosquito, her eyes magnified by thick lenses.

"I hate mosquitoes," Storm mumbled under her breath.

Valerie was next. She closed her eyes, took a deep, zen-like cleansing breath, and released it. She did not make a sound as the nurse administered the injections.

Storm watched. "Harrumph!" she huffed, still not liking the idea of getting shots.

It was Ebony's turn next. Just as she'd done with Kyloni and Valerie, the nurse took a cotton ball with alcohol and cleaned the area. She rubbed Ebony's arm.

"Ow, ow, ow!" she screeched, pulling away from the cold alcohol swab.

The nurse shook her head and laughed.

"It's only the cotton ball. I haven't even given you the injections yet." To divert her attention away from the needle she asked, "Can you reach over and grab that Band-Aid for me? Thank you." As she reached across the tray, the nurse managed to give the vaccines before Ebony could protest again. It was over so quickly, she didn't have time for more dramatics.

"Oh, is that it?" Ebony giggled, "I didn't feel a thing." She turned to Storm. "Hey, brat. It's your turn."

"I want Yalani to go next!" Storm challenged, pointing a finger. Yalani, the "scaredy-cat," was lurking as far away from the tray of needles as possible.

"Okay, Storm. Yalani can go instead." Miss Cherie turned to find her hiding in a corner of the room. There she was studying a poster on the wall of the human body's muscular and nervous systems. "It's your turn."

Yalani stood silent, not moving an inch. She'd hoped she'd been forgotten. She hated needles; just the sight of them made her want to run screaming from the room. She swallowed the lump in her throat with a gulp. Last time this happened was five years ago with a rather embarrassing incident where she had to be restrained.

"No, no let Storm go before me. I—I want to go last." she stammered, nervously. "Storm, you don't mind, do you?" Her eyes were pleading.

Storm felt sorry for her, but not that sorry. She gave Yalani's request some thought and quickly made her decision. Nope.

"I want you to go first." A devilish grin played upon her lips as she tried to keep a straight face. This time she really was being a brat. She knew there was a possibility of a funny epic fail if it involved Yalani being scared.

Cherie leaned over and whispered something into Storm's ear.

Storm's face lit up with a gigantic smile. "Really?"

"Really." Cherie agreed; she knew she had her.

"Anything I want?" Storm questioned, already running through a mental list of things on her Amazon wish list.

"Yes, Storm, anything you want." The deal was struck and sealed.

Storm walked confidently over to the nurse, rolled up her sleeves, cracked her knuckles, then playfully struck a warrior yoga pose she'd learned in their weekly yoga classes. Whatever deal she'd made with Cherie, her mind was completely changed. She took one look at the needles and said, "Okay, lady, let's do this!"

The nurse quickly administered the shots before she could change her mind. Storm sat fidgeting a little, as she waited and waited, wondering when this was going to be over with already. "I'm ready, let's get the ball rolling!"

"Young lady," the nurse said, "I've already given you the injections. You're all finished."

Storm smiled sheepishly. After all her protesting, she'd felt only a slight sting, thinking it was the alcohol swab. She grinned, happy with the secret deal she'd made with Cherie.

"Oh." She hopped down from the chair next to the examining table. "Ya-la-ni. It's your turn," she taunted. From her back pocket, she pulled out her cell phone and pressed record. This was going to be good.

Yalani took one baby step at a time toward the nurse. Her thoughts whirled, and her feet felt as if they were trapped in thick, gooey slime. She paused as the nurse turned to her, smiling, a needle held in each hand. Everything seemed to be in slow motion.

"Come on, Yalani ... Let's get you taken care of ..."

She was nearly to the nurse when she felt the first sign of dizziness. *Oh no. Oh no, no, no.* She was not going to faint and embarrass herself again. She wavered and swayed, closing her eyes and bringing a hand to her forehead. Ebony's shrill voice snapped her back to reality.

"Like, oh my god, is this going to happen every single time she gets scared. *So* boring." Ebony flipped her hair, studied her nails, and added, "Oh no. I chipped my nail polish. Now I'll have to go back to the nail salon and get them done again. Shoot."

Cherie flushed angrily, finally addressing the "mean girl" attitude.

"We are a team. And your team member needs your help, Ebony. You're seventeen years old, the oldest in the group. The other girls look up to you, and you have a responsibility to set the example."

"Yes, but I—" Ebony tried to speak, but Cherie kept talking. She wasn't finished with her lecture.

"As a team, we won the 'Good Citizenship' award. Do you remember what that meant?" She kept talking, not waiting for an answer. "Respect, kindness, friendliness, helping our fellow man … Remember those? Oh, and being a role model. And we are a team. And look where it's gotten us!"

"But, but—" Ebony made another attempt to get a word in edgewise. She continued, cutting her off again. Oh boy! Ebony had really gotten her started. This was going to take a while. There was nothing else for them to do but wait it out until she was finished with her tongue-lashing.

"What more could you ask for? You are an incredibly lucky group of young ladies. We're going to Africa in a few days. Africa. How many people in their lifetime will get such an opportunity? And furthermore, who do you think you are—?"

Several tugs on her shirt sleeve caught her attention. She stopped midsentence, coming face to face with Yalani.

"I'm finished, Miss Cherie. I kept my promise. Ebony helped me." Yalani turned to Ebony and mouthed a "*thank you.*"

"How? Wait, what? Did she? Is this true? You're not pulling my leg, are you?" Cherie was surprised. It was not like Ebony to think of anyone but herself.

"It's true. Look. I got it on video." Miss Cherie leaned over Storm's shoulder and watched the video from beginning to end. To her disbelief, Ebony was truly helping Yalani to the nurse's station after she had nearly fainted.

Cherie turned to Ebony, apologized, and then thanked her, adding, "This is the perfect example of what teamwork is all about."

Ebony blushed, uncomfortable. Helping others was not something she did often. All the positive attention made her feel all weird and ticklish inside. The nurse interrupted, snapping her out of her thoughts. There were more patients waiting to be seen. She passed out what looked like yellow postcards to each one of them.

"Hold on to these. They're especially important for your trip. They are your immunization cards. Keep them safe along with your passports. They're proof that you've been vaccinated against several diseases including the flu, yellow fever, and typhoid, which can cause illness from eating contaminated food and drinking unclean water. Also, these pills are for protection against malaria from mosquito bites. The instructions are on the bottle. You'll take these starting today, the entire time you're in Africa, and seven days after your return. Oh, and I'd stick to bottled water. It's safest; I suggest you even brush your teeth with it."

With that last bit of advice, they gathered their belongings and headed toward the exit. Cherie collected their passports and vaccine cards as they walked through the door. She would keep the documents safe until it was time to board their flight. They were nearly ready for the journey with one last thing to do before leaving for Africa: shopping!

CHAPTER 4

CHECKLIST CHECK

—

"In 100 feet, turn right, and then turn left," the navigation system announced. "You have reached your destination." Miss Cherie carefully steered the vehicle into the parking lot of the Camper's Paradise Superstore. Slowing, she found a parking space near the front entrance. People turned and stared at the Wildlife Diva's sports vehicle. The entire SUV was covered in a jungle ecosystem decal with wild animals that were considered endangered species. An elephant, gorilla, tiger, panda, koala bear, and their motto, *"answering the call of the wild #DivaStyle,"* decorated each side of the van.

All the added attention was new to them. Usually, life at Ravenswing Academy was quiet. They had few visitors, and even fewer family members. Two of the five girls had no family at all. The other three had living relatives, but well, let's just say it was best that those particular members of their families stayed away.

The girls created their own little family among themselves, forming what Miss Cherie hoped would become lifelong bonds of friendship and becoming as close as sisters. They borrowed each other's clothing and sometimes argued like siblings.

As soon as Miss Cherie put the car in park, they were out of the vehicle and the nine and eleven-year-olds raced toward the front door of the store. The older girls followed behind. Excited, they chatted away. It was their first time visiting the camping superstore.

Taking Storm by the hand, mostly to keep her out of trouble, Miss Cherie walked through the sliding glass doors. They were amazed. Every inch of the store seemed to be covered with different types of sporting equipment. Hanging from the ceiling were tents, row boats, hammocks, bicycles, skateboards, and more. There was anything you could imagine from outdoor to indoor sports, camping gear, and water sports. You name it, they had it.

At Cherie's request, Valerie pulled up a checklist of items on her phone and typed in the search field, "Gorilla Safari Checklist."

The search engine returned "Gorilla Trekking Packing List: All You Need for Gorilla Tracking."

She touched the link and the list of items appeared.

GORILLA TREKKING PACKING LIST

The packing list below is a mere guideline as you may have your own preferences.

- One or two long sleeved shirts
- Three short sleeved shirts
- Two or three pairs of lightweight slacks or trousers that can dry quickly
- One pair of shorts
- One sweater, sweatshirt, or hoodie
- One waterproof and windproof jacket
- One pair of gardening gloves
- Durable waterproof walking boots or heavy-soled rain boots (Pants should be tucked into socks and boots while trekking.)
- Pair of sports sandals or shower shoes
- Wide brim hat or cap with a visor for sun protection
- Sleepwear
- Underwear
- Lightweight wool socks
- ~~Swimsuit and a plastic bag for storage~~

With a couple touches of her phone screen, Valerie shared the list to everyone's phone. Each dinged and pinged with message alerts.

"Okay, you should have the list on your phones."

Cherie read the shared message. "We won't be needing swimsuits. You can cross that off the list; there will be no time for a swim. All the other things on the list are must-haves."

She cleared her throat. She had an announcement. "Ahem. Before we get started, I have a surprise for everyone."

A surprise? She had their attention. "We've been given a stipend." She held up a hand to quiet them from asking a dozen questions. "It's like an allowance." Allowances they understood.

"Just how much of an 'allowance' are we talking about?" Ebony asked, raising an eyebrow. To Ebony, nothing in life is better than money and shopping. Well, maybe boys. And clothes and makeup. Oh, and her Instagram followers.

"It's just a little something-something," Miss Cherie teased, pulling from her handbag gift card envelopes for each of them. "We were granted a gift of five hundred dollars each—"

High-pitched screams and squeals of delight erupted from five girls. Customers and employees turned to look at them. The sudden ear-piercing outburst startled them.

"Quiet down." Cherie chuckled; she'd hadn't expected such an overblown response. She was a little embarrassed and should have done this before entering the store. She handed an envelope to each girl.

"Now listen, we don't have to spend every dime, Ebony," Cherie said pointedly as the girl greedily snatched the envelope from her fingers. "Let's be penny-wise. This money has to last the entire trip. Storm, I'll hold on to yours." She turned in a circle looking for her.

Storm had wandered over to a display of camping equipment. Wide-eyed she stared curiously, trying to figure out how each item was used.

Ebony and Yalani, now besties, moseyed over to see what she was up to.

Storm grabbed something from the display case that caught her interest. "Whoa! Look at this!"

"Put that back; you don't even know what it is." Yalani cautioned.

"It's a hat. See." Storm placed the plastic "hat" on top of her head, admiring it in the mirror from several angles. "*Whoa*, look at this. It has a flip top. I can let my hair out of the top. Check it out." She opened the lid and two large afro puffs, ribbons and all, poked through the opening. When she closed it, soft puffs of hair resembling mouse ears disappeared beneath.

Ebony grabbed the same hat and read the tag attached to it and chuckled. She motioned for Yalani to come over. Reading the label, she snickered.

"Storm. You are not going to like this." She giggled, "It's a—" She could barely get the words out, laughter overtaking her. "It's a toilet seat lid!" Ebony roared with laughter and Yalani joined in, cackling loudly.

"*A toilet seat lid!*" Storm bellowed. "You mean people put their butts on this to go potty?"

Laughing so hard they could not answer her question but only nod yes, tears rolled down their cheeks.

"Yuck, phooey, disgusting! I need a shower, that's just—that's just nasty." Storm shuddered. She turned on Ebony and Yalani. "You guys stop laughing. It's not funny!" Their laughter felt as if they were mocking her. She angrily snatched the lid off. She did not like being made fun of.

Valerie and Kyloni came to the rescue, whisking Storm away as fast and as far away from the laughing duo. She glared back at them, vowing payback.

Valerie removed a tan safari hat from its display and placed it upon her head.

"Much, much better," she said, her voice barely above a whisper. "Now this is perfect for you." She eyed Storm's brand-new hat approvingly and chose one for herself. "This is just right for the rainforest."

Kyloni complimented the two on their choice of hats. "Nice Shola Pith hats. You know, these hats were once made from the dried-up, milk-white, spongey insides of the Shola tree. They're found in the forests of Northern India. Great insulators from extreme heat." She was met with blank stares.

She waved her hand, then pushed up her eyeglasses. "Oh, never mind that. These are most likely made from Styrofoam plastic anyways. Look what I've found for our future entomologist." She handed several items to Storm, "Here you go, little bug lover."

"A bug catcher and binoculars! Cool!" she shrieked with delight. She truly did love insects. She placed the binoculars around her neck. A magnifying glass and butterfly net completed her outfit. She beamed, looking very much like the adventurer and explorer. She couldn't wait to catch bugs, spiders, and butterflies in Africa.

* * *

After a couple hours of shopping, everyone walked away with their checklist finished. As they stood in line to make their purchases, they talked eagerly about their trip to Africa. In line behind them was a woman with a small child listening closely to their conversations.

"Pardon me," the woman interrupted. "I couldn't help but overhear. What exactly is a Wildlife Diva? I've never heard of this organization before."

"We're going to Africa," Storm blurted out.

"Storm, manners please. Introduce yourself properly," Miss Cherie corrected her.

Part of the agreement made with Doctor Khambrel was that the girls must have outstanding behavior and character. They were the faces representing WAR, or the Wildlife Authority Rescue. It was important that they be polite, well-mannered, and courteous.

"Oops, my bad." She started over. "Hi, my name is Storm, and I am a member of The Wildlife Divas." Reaching out she shook the lady's hand.

"It's a pleasure to meet you, Storm. I'm Jessica, and this is my son, Jeremy." Three-year-old Jeremy hid behind his mother's skirt, shyly peeking out from behind her. He grinned around the thumb stuck in his mouth. They exited through the sliding glass doors and stood in front of the store to continue their conversation.

"I overheard you saying you were going to Africa. How exciting! What country will you visit? Tell me more about your trip. What is it that you do?"

The bombardment of questions left Storm briefly confused.

"Well, I, we're going to, umm …" She looked to Miss Cherie for help.

"We are wildlife ambassadors sworn to protect the lives of animals that are on the critically endangered species list," Miss Cherie stated. "Animals are losing their habitats to deforestation.

Some are losing their habitat because people need more places to live and as the population grows, they spill over into their areas where gorillas live. Others are being poached, kidnapped, and sold to private owners. And still there are other species of wildlife that are being hunted to the brink of extinction."

She did not pause for a breath and continued. "And yes, we're on our way to the East African Nation of Uganda. Our first assignment will take us to the Bwindi Impenetrable Forest to help bring attention to the plight of mountain gorillas, where the population has fallen due to these exact reasons. We want future generations to witness these magnificent and gentle creatures in rainforests which are their natural habits, not just behind stone enclosures in zoos." She loved seeing their faces filled with interest and understanding.

"Well, this seems to be a very noble cause," Jessica said, impressed. "What can I do to help? And my son too?" Still hiding behind his mother, Jeremy peeked out, his thumb still planted firmly in his mouth. "Would you like to help the Gorillas in Africa?" she asked.

Removing his thumb, Jeremy said in his baby voice, "Yes, Mommy. I help 'rillas."

Miss Cherie sent Kyloni racing to the van where she grabbed a stuffed animal from the trunk and raced back. "If you purchase our stuffed gorilla," she continued, "a portion of the money is donated to the veterinary organizations that care for the gorillas in the rainforest."

Kyloni kneeled to meet Jeremy's gaze, her glasses sliding down to the tip of her nose.

"His scientific name is 'Gorilla beringei beringei,'" she started, "Gorillas are classified as primates belonging to the group of animals called mammals. Dinosaurs roamed the earth and were obliterated by fiery gases from a colossal meteor roughly sixty-five million years ago." She gestured to the sky. Jeremy squinted his eyes as he followed her arm movements. "Mammals became the dominant species. The first true mammals evolved during the Jurassic era two hundred million years ago—"

Jeremy stared, wide-eyed, taking several sucks of his thumb. "*Mine!*" he interrupted, reaching for the toy. He ignored her recount, as any reasonable three-year-old would, of the sudden mass extinction of dinosaurs.

"Hm, right. 'Mine.' Okay, yeah," she said, accepting his disinterest. She instead used the toy gorilla's arm to tickle Jeremy. He giggled and squealed with delight. "Here you go. He's all yours."

Finally removing a wet thumb from his mouth, Jeremy grabbed the stuffed animal, hugging it tightly to his chest. He tried feeding it with his thumb. They all laughed at how adorably cute he was. Social media expert Ebony recorded the encounter.

Jessica asked for a group photo. Valerie, with her selfie stick, had them gather close together and raised it far above them. "On the count of three, everyone, let's say gorillas. One, two, three!"

They all shouted, "*Gorillas!*"

Ebony snapped several pics. "And if it's okay, let's take one more with your phone, Jessica. I want you to remember the Wildlife Divas." She took the photos and added, "Don't forget to follow us on Instagram, Twitter, and Facebook." They waved their goodbyes.

"Have a safe trip, Divas!"

It was time to go home, get their suitcases packed, and get a good night's sleep. Tomorrow they would leave for Uganda.

CHAPTER 5

JOURNEY TO AFRICA

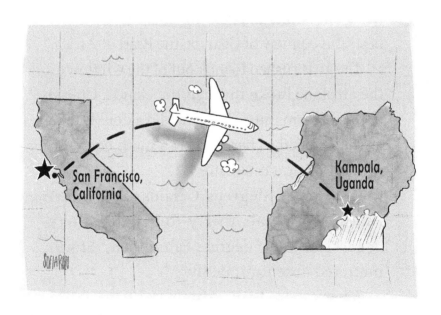

The pilot made the announcement over the loudspeaker. "We are now making our final approach to the Entebbe-Kampala International Airport." His voice sounded as if he were talking through a walkie-talkie radio. "Please return to your seats and fasten your seat belts. Put your seats in the upright position and your tray tables away. We will be landing in about twenty minutes. It's a beautiful day in Kampala, the temperature is seventeen degrees Celsius, and the current local time is seven o'clock in the morning. Thank you for flying our airline and have a wonderful visit in the beautiful country of Uganda, the Pearl of Africa."

The girls rushed to look out of the window as the airplane broke through the clouds. Cherie noticed Storm mumbling and did a double take as she listened to her convert a math equation without using a calculator.

"Seventeen degrees Celsius. Seventeen times two equals thirty-four, plus thirty equals sixty-four degrees Fahrenheit," Storm muttered absentmindedly.

Cherie raised an eyebrow in surprise and made a mental note to ask her about it later. For now, they were all too excited as they gazed at the lush green countryside, trees, and mountains appearing below. There was the city with many buildings and homes scattered about. The streets were filled with people moving in all directions, like tiny ants busily going about their work.

Ebony slept unfazed, her pink, blinged-out "Diva at Rest" sleep mask firmly in place over her eyes. She snored loudly!

"Look, you're missing it! We're almost there! Wake up, Ebony!" Storm shook the back of Ebony's seat, trying to rouse her from sleep and stop that horrendous snoring.

"Go away, brat, leave me alone," Ebony grumbled. She turned over, pulling the blanket up around her shoulders and tucking it beneath her chin. She continued to snore.

Yalani looked mortified. When trying to help Ebony re-tuck her blanket, she slapped her hand away. Yalani, embarrassed, looked at Storm who shrugged her shoulders and went back to looking out the window, gazing at the beautiful countryside. She pointed.

"Look, the ocean!"

Kyloni and Valerie were comparing facts about Uganda on their phones when Storm's comment got their attention. Kyloni looked over the top of her glasses, bringing her phone inches away from her face. She peered at the screen, retrieving facts about the "ocean."

"For your information, *that* is not an ocean. It so happens to be the largest freshwater lake on the African continent."

"A lake? No way! It looks like an ocean. See, there's a beach right there." Storm reported what she saw, her breath fogging up the window.

Sure enough, there was a hotel on the lake's shoreline. Storm pressed her face against the window for a better view. She could make out umbrellas and beach chairs that looked to be the size of doll furniture from her sky-high view.

"That is Lake Victoria, named after Queen Victoria of the United Kingdom," she said after verifying the information on her phone.

"Who? Queen of what?" Storm asked, still focused on the lake.

With a mock British accent, Valerie answered. "The Queen of England. Would you like tea and crumpets, my dear?"

Storm liked Valerie's fake accent. "Cheerio," she added, giggling.

Kyloni continued, ignoring the interruption. "The area of the lake is 26,600 square miles and it borders three African nations: Tanzania, Kenya, and of course Uganda. Interesting fact here. The River Nile originates here in Uganda and flows north through several African countries, eventually flowing through Egypt and finally pouring into the Mediterranean Sea. An amazing 4,132 miles. You learn something new every day."

The airplane glided above the lake as it reduced speed. It seemed they would land in the water when they felt a sudden thud and a screeching sound as the rubber tires made contact with the pavement. It slowed with great force as the engines reversed causing the plane to shake, rattle, and shimmy.

The flight attendant picked of the microphone, "Welcome to Kampala. Please remain seated until we come to a complete stop and the pilot has turned off the 'No Seat Belts' sign. Be careful when opening overhead compartments as things may have shifted during the flight. Make sure to gather all your personal belongings, laptops, phones, jackets, and glasses. Thank you for flying with us and again, welcome to Uganda."

The plane came to a halt and the "No Seat Belts" sign went off with a ding. Cherie, Storm, a now awake Ebony, Yalani, Valerie, and Kyloni looked at one another and burst into a gleeful moment of laughter. They'd made it. Their first trip outside of the United States. It had taken twenty-six long hours and two plane changes, one which sent them racing across the airport, nearly missing their connecting flight. They gathered up their belongings excitedly, chattering as they got off the plane. The team made their way down the stairs to the airstrip, leaving Miss Cherie and Storm behind.

Oops, there was a problem. During the bumpy landing, some of Storm's belongings fell and tumbled beneath the seat in front of her.

"Hurry along Storm, we need to exit the plane."

"Coming. Some of my things fell over when we landed." She strained reaching beneath the seat to retrieve the items, which were just out of arm's reach. She got down on all fours and reached under the seat. Got it! She gasped and looked around frantically.

"C'mon, young lady, we need to get off the plane. Did you find your things?"

Storm did not answer; she was in a panic. She crawled along the floor, her heart pounding in her chest. She crawled from one seat to the next, growing more and more frantic.

At home, as they had packed for the trip, there was a big fight with lots of tears and pouting. The argument ended finally when Miss Cherie surrendered. Storm had reminded her several times that "you said I could bring anything I wanted. You promised?" It was true, she did promise and now was obligated to keep her word. So, Storm won the battle and was able to bring her prized possession.

Slowly she stood up and slid into the airplane seat. She frowned, her bottom lip trembled, her honey-brown eyes filled with tears as she looked up at Miss Cherie.

She held in her hands her new bug atrium. It's little cage door sat wide open. Inside there was nothing. It was empty. Storm cried.

"She's not here. She got out!" Storm whined and sniffled, wiping her runny nose with the back of her sleeve. "Miss Cherie, she's not here. She's gone." She repeated, this time wailing, "She's gone ... I can't find my spider!"

CHAPTER 6

SPINDERELLA

Storm slumped down in her seat. Folding her arms firmly across her chest, she refused to move despite Miss Cherie's trying to coax her off the plane. They would find her spider, she promised, but first they needed to leave the plane.

She wiped away another teardrop with the back of her shirt sleeve. Several of the flight attendants gathered around. One handed her tissues to blow her snotty nose. She was not leaving this plane without her spider.

The flight crew took pity on her and offered to look one more time. This was precisely the reason why insects and rodents were not allowed in the cabin with passengers but could be stored underneath in the storage area of the plane where the larger suitcases were kept.

The captain made an exception to the rule just this one time. Storm had given him a convincing argument. Who could resist her adorable, brown face and those eyes? Now look at what happened.

One last time, they searched the aircraft. One flight attendant, the one to handed her the tissues, did not participate. She seemed deathly afraid of spiders and stood atop a seat, swatting at invisible spiders or any object brushing against her.

The second search revealed nothing. There was no spider on this plane. They looked beneath the surrounding seats, looking in tiny nooks and crannies where a spider could possibly hide. No luck. She was gone.

There was no choice; they had to leave the plane. The aircraft needed to be cleaned and new passengers would board for the next flight.

Outside, there was a celebration. Drums beat rhythmically. People were clapping and cheering, except for one odd sound. Someone was screaming. It was Ebony!

"Spinderella!" Tears forgotten, Storm sprinted to the front of the plane, dashed out the doorway and down the stairs, skipping two at a time. She reached the bottom, breathing heavily. She blinked several times, confused, trying to make sense of the chaos in front of her and doubled over, clutching her belly, laughter overtaking her.

* * *

Moments before, Ebony had been first to leave the aircraft. She made her way down the stairs with Yalani, her most adoring fan, close on her heels. Being that she was Instagram famous, Ebony assumed all the people waiting for their family members must be there for her. She waved hello and smiled brightly to anyone looking her way. She reached the bottom of the stairs and was greeted by a young man about her age. And he was cute! She blushed, batting her eyelashes as he approached.

"*Nabbubi*," he said, pointing directly at her.

"N'bui to you too," she said, making an obvious attempt to flirt. She whispered to Yalani, "I bet that means he thinks I'm cute."

Yalani watched adoringly. She wanted to be popular like her.

"No, *nabbubi*. Look," he leaned in toward her, getting closer.

Ebony turned her head for what she believed would be a kiss on the cheek in greeting, but instead, he tugged at something tangled in her hair.

"See, ma'am? *Nabbubi*," he held it near her face. "Spider."

Ebony's mouth formed a perfect "O" as she screamed in terror, her nightmare come true. Storm's pet tarantula!

Her once perfectly styled hairdo was now a tangled mess as she smacked, pulled, and swatted wildly.

"Get it off! Get it away from me!" Ebony shrieked. She twisted and turned, jumped up and down, and ran in circles to get away from the hairy eight-legged beast.

A crowd noticed the commotion and turned to watch. It looked as if Ebony were performing a dance. A man with a drum made of a hollowed-out tree trunk with an animal skin stretched tightly across dropped a beat that matched her movements. The people began to clap and joined in with her dance performance. What a party!

A still chuckling Storm approached the young man.

"Spinderella, there you are, naughty girl. Where were you going?" Storm cooed, gently handling the pet tarantula she'd raised from a newly hatched spiderling. "Of all the people you could have taken a ride on, you chose Ebony. You could have been hurt. Poor baby. Did she scare you?"

She eased Spinderella back into her bug catcher, where she latched the door securely. Her favorite pet was now safe and sound. She turned to the young man with a beaming smile and thanked him. The flight crew looked on from the doorway. She held up the bug catcher and thanked them too.

"Found her. Thanks for your help!" she shouted.

Ebony sat on the sidewalk, overcome with exhaustion. Yalani fanned her face and tried smoothing her wayward hairs back in place with little success. Not only was her hair a mess, but her makeup was ruined as well. Black mascara tears streaked down her face.

"C'mon, let's get you cleaned up. The bathroom's right over here." Valerie and Yalani helped Ebony to her feet and escorted her to the restroom with Kyloni trailing closely behind.

"You were quite lucky, Ebony," Kyloni explained. "Tarantulas protect themselves with urticating hairs, *urtica* being the Latin word, which means 'nettle.'" Using her index finger, she pushed her glasses off the tip of her nose and half-laughed, half-snorted. "Actually, that's a misnomer; they're more like bristles than hairs. And when threatened by a predator, they kick these barbed bristles off their abdomens with their rear legs, causing a cloud of stinging needle-like hairs to embed themselves in your eyes and skin, causing a great amount of discomfort and pain."

Ebony shot Kyloni an angry stare, stopping her in her tracks.

"Uh oh, I don't think I'm needed here." Kyloni waited for a response, but Ebony continued to stare at her. "No? Okay, I'll just go away." She did a 180 and hurried back in the direction where Storm and Cherie stood, greeting a man with a sign.

The man holding the sign "Wildlife Divas" was Kevin Byarugaba, their official gorilla trekking safari guide to the Bwindi Impenetrable Forest National Park.

"*Mujebaleko.* Hello!" He greeted them in both Luganda and English. Although Swahili and English are the official languages of Uganda, Luganda is spoken by millions.

Cherie stepped forward to shake Kevin's hand, introducing herself, as the girls joined her. "*Mu-je-ba-le-ko,*" she repeated. "It's a pleasure to finally meet you in person, Kevin. I'm Cherie." They'd corresponded by email and social media to coordinate their trip. "Allow me to introduce you to the rest of the Wildlife Divas team."

Cherie introduced them in order from the oldest to the youngest. "This is Ebony, Kyloni,

Valerie, Yalani, and Storm." Ebony nodded, her face clean and presentable after quickly touching up her makeup. Kyloni waved and pushed up her glasses. Valerie said nothing and just looked at the ground. Yalani curtsied while Storm took a bow.

"It is my pleasure to meet such a lovely group of young ladies," he said. They beamed at the compliment. "We just need to grab your luggage, get it packed on the jeeps, and we'll be on our way. We have a bit of a ride ahead of us. Let's get started."

* * *

They took the short walk to the baggage claim area to retrieve their luggage. Ebony took the opportunity to approach Storm alone so she could threaten her properly.

"Storm, you brat. Thanks to you I made a fool of myself." Ebony whispered dangerously. "I'm going to get you for this … Just wait. When you least expect it—expect it!" She was not one to forget an insult.

"I'm sorry, but it wasn't my fault you were acting like a fool." Storm retorted; she wasn't taking the blame. "Her cage tumbled over when the plane landed. I didn't know where she'd gone. I thought I'd lost her forever."

Storm removed the young tarantula from her carrier and cooed, "Isn't that right, Spinderella? We wouldn't want you to get out again and hitch another ride on Ebony, would we?"

Storm made eye contact with Ebony as Spinderella crawled over her hand and up her arm before capturing her and placing her back in the cage. There was a mischievous smile on her lips.

Ebony shuddered. The innocent gesture sent a clear message: don't mess with me. She hurried away in a huff. Paranoid, she brushed her hand across each shoulder to make sure there were no spiders there.

She turned her wrath on the baggage handler, whom she felt was mishandling her five designer suitcases too roughly.

"Be careful! Don't drop it," she protested, taking her misdirected anger out on him. "There are things inside that are fragile and can break. No, no, put that one down, I'll carry it myself. Oh my god!"

By the look on the man's face, he was not happy with such a demanding, entitled individual with such a ridiculous amount of luggage. He dropped the bags and stalked away in frustration, leaving her struggling with her own belongings.

There were two transport vans waiting for them, one carrying their luggage and the other carrying the Wildlife Divas Team.

All six climbed aboard the van; they all fit comfortably. They began the long, eight-hour drive to their campground.

First, they drove through the streets of Kampala. Hundreds upon hundreds of people walked the streets of the city, going about their busy mornings.

"It's very crowded here as you can see. There are more than 1.5 million people who live here," Kevin explained.

Bicycles and motorbikes, called *boda bodas,* were everywhere. By the thousands it seemed. Buses lined every street, creating stop-and-go traffic. When they stopped at an intersection, several children ran up to their van to sell water, lukewarm soft drinks, and unfamiliar meat on sticks.

Kevin continued, "For some families, this is their only means of income. These children give the money to their families."

Finally, out of the city, paved roads turned into the red clay roadways, as they made their way through the countryside. Women and young girls their ages dressed in brightly colored outfits, and they carried large items—like huge jugs of neck-breaking water containers and bundles of wood at least ten feet long—upon their heads.

Kevin explained that many of the young girls walked several miles every day to retrieve fresh water for cooking, bathing, and washing clothes, and if their families could afford, they would walk to school. Many walked the miles barefoot, being so poor they could not afford shoes.

They were beginning to realize how lucky they were. And although they lived in the richest country in the world, their neighborhood was one of the poorest in their hometown of San Francisco. Yet even their poor living conditions were better than some people living in Ugandan villages they passed on the way to Bwindi. They did not know people in some part of the other side of the world lived under worse conditions than theirs.

Many of the homes they passed along the way were made of red, clay bricks. The Divas could not imagine walking for miles to go to school, nor walking for miles to gather water every single day. They were quiet and thoughtful as they rambled along the bumpy country roads.

Animals roamed freely. Goats, herds of sheep, and big horned cows called Ankole Cattle—with horns reaching up to eight feet wide—walked along the roadside. As they traveled, the land turned into green rolling hills and mountains.

After several hours, they stopped for a break. The drivers pulled onto the side of the road overlooking a small lake, the mountains in the distance shrouded in mist. It was beautiful, lush and green. They were close and would soon arrive, they were told. For the rest of their trip, they talked, napped, told stories, laughed and played games like "I Spy" with Storm asking several times, "Are we there yet?" until they finally arrived.

* * *

The posted sign read "Bwindi Impenetrable National Forest." The Wildlife Divas Adventure Team stumbled out of the van, yawning and stretching like cats awakening from a long nap. The first part of their journey was over—getting there. It had taken a total of two whole days of traveling to arrive from San Francisco. And even though they were exhausted, they could not contain their excitement. They were in Africa.

They were met by a woman named Sharon, the hotel staff, and other members. Some staff took their luggage to their rooms while other staff members guided them to the restaurant. This is where they would meet for breakfast and all other meals would be served. This is where they could have African tea, a tea made with freshly pounded ginger and milk. A coffee bar was available any time, day or night.

They were assigned bedrooms with two team members in each room. Kyloni and Valerie would bunk together. Ebony and Yalani too, and of course, Cherie bunked with Storm and Spinderella, mostly to keep her out of trouble and away from Ebony.

They were amazed as they reached the campground. It looked very much like a jungle tree house nestled high among the trees.

They were happily surprised to find their rooms were beautifully decorated. Fluffy, white down comforters and sheer white nets covered each bed, so inviting they wanted to immediately crawl in and fall asleep. It was explained that the nets were not just pretty but were to keep them protected from insects that carry diseases, like mosquitoes, as they slept.

Curiously, Storm followed the hotel host around the room as she explained how things worked.

"The shower," Sharon explained, "must be allowed to run for five minutes to allow the water to warm up." She added that when they come for breakfast, they were to bring their keys and leave them in a basket upon entering the restaurant.

After the brief instructions, Storm sauntered next door to Valerie and Kyloni's room.

"Hey, what are you guys doing?" she asked, peeking her head just inside their front door.

Kyloni began by pushing up her glasses from the tip of her nose. "We are attempting to understand this digital Bluetooth apparatus. This technology is quite fascinating."

Storm slammed the door shut mid-explanation. Off she went to see Ebony and Yalani.

She knocked first and when no one answered, she entered the room.

"Hey, brat, what are you doing in our room? Get out already." Ebony's shrill voice exclaimed as she folded one arm across her chest and pointed toward the door, "Get to steppin'!"

Yalani followed Ebony's lead. "Yeah, get to steppin'. Go back to your own room!" she cried, mimicking Ebony's stance. Dejected, Storm's frowning face disappeared from the doorway as she closed it. She quickly reopened the door, slid her head back in, stuck out her tongue, and—slamming the door shut with a bang—trotted back to her and Cherie's room.

They were advised to unpack and shower while a light dinner was prepared. Near the end of the hallway, the showers were actually outdoors with walls high enough to give privacy and a surprisingly beautiful view of mountains in the distance. Afterwards, they took a quick nap then made their way down to the dining area for a light meal and orientation.

Met by the setting sun, they were guided outside and sat in a semicircle next to a brightly lit campfire.

There they relaxed and talked about the best part of their trip so far. Soon they spotted Kevin, their gorilla trekking guide. They watched as he made his way toward them and stood in front of the campfire. He prepared to make a big announcement.

CHAPTER 7

RULES RULE

Kevin Byarugaba stood in the center of the group. The girls stopped talking and gave him their full attention.

"Tomorrow morning, we will start our gorilla trek into the jungle." He motioned to a path leading into the forest, "But first, we need to go over information that is of vital importance to your assignment, the reason why we are here, and a few critical rules before we get started." He scanned their faces, which were filled with nervous excitement.

"As you know, you were asked to come on this particular assignment to help bring attention to the plight of the critically endangered mountain gorillas here in Uganda. Poachers are kidnapping baby gorillas and selling them for large sums of money. This practice is highly illegal, and it is our sworn duty to protect these animals." Kevin continued. "Due to poaching and habitat loss, there are less than nine hundred mountain gorillas left on the entire planet. They live nowhere else in the world other than here in the African nations of Uganda, Rwanda, and the Democratic Republic of Congo."

His next words were especially important.

"It can be exciting and fun, but you must remember at all times that this is a dangerous mission. So, it's important that you pay attention to what we are about to discuss. In the forest there are wild animals. Some you've never encountered before in your lives. And then there are the poachers. We asked you here to help save baby mountain gorillas. The poachers have been quite active hunting, setting traps, and kidnapping them. They are armed and they are dangerous. I cannot stress enough the danger they present. I need you to listen carefully, and do not be afraid to ask questions. Your lives depend on it."

He ended this portion of the speech with a solemn face. He looked at each member of the team, noting if they were paying attention. He needed them to understand the seriousness of his words, then said, "Now, the rules."

Kevin paced back and forth in front of the Divas. He held up one finger. "Rule Number One! This rule is the most important of all. *Don't! Run!*"

They looked at one another, wide-eyed and a bit confused. That couldn't be right. Did he just say "don't run?"

Timidly, Yalani raised her hand to ask a question.

"Kevin, when you say don't run … Don't run from what?"

"Well, the gorillas of course. I know this goes against your instinct when threatened, but if you find yourself face to face with a gorilla, if one charges toward you, you should not run away. Stand your ground or better yet, assume a squatting position with your head lowered. Gorillas see this posture as submission, sort of like an apology in gorilla language." He gave them an example by sitting and squatting, head down. "Like this." he said, allowing the information to sink in.

"For the most part, gorillas are gentle creatures, but if you run, the gorilla takes it as a sign of aggression, and he will chase you, maybe even strike you," he explained.

Yalani swallowed hard, a lump of fear stuck in her throat, momentarily speechless.

"S-strike me? Kevin, do you mean hit me?" Her voice was barely louder than a whisper. She fought back tears. She found this truly frightening.

Cherie walked over to Yalani placing her arm around her shoulders, comforting her.

"There's no need to be scared, right, Kevin? We have our guides and the gorilla trackers to keep us safe!"

"Absolutely," replied Kevin. "There is nothing to worry about. Jimbo will be your personal guide. He's the most experienced and will keep you safe from harm." Kevin assured her.

Yalani sniffled, pulled a tissue from her pocket, and blew her nose.

"Okay, if you say so," she said unhappily. She glanced at Kevin, giving him a weak smile, still doubtful he could keep her safe from harm.

"Brilliant," Kevin said and continued.

He held up two fingers.

"Rule number two: speak quietly. When we encounter the gorillas, we must speak in a soft voice. Whisper. That means no yelling and no screaming in excitement or fear. Yelling and speaking too loudly can be taken as a threat."

Three fingers.

"Rule number three! No sudden movements. Meaning no jumping, no skipping, and especially no running." This time, his eyes came to rest on Storm. "This can also be seen as a sign of aggression."

"Tonight, I want you to get plenty of rest. In the morning after breakfast, we will get started. You'll need your backpacks and supplies. Remember to dress properly. Mornings are cool here. I wish you a good night."

The Wildlife Divas were dismissed for the night. Cheri led them to their rooms and helped them prepare for bed. They talked among themselves and watched the video Valerie recorded during orientation so they could review the rules together.

They were as ready as they could ever be. They climbed into their beds, pulled their mosquito nets closed, crawled beneath the covers, and quickly fell asleep.

The rainforest, with its many mysteries, awaited them.

* * *

Somewhere deep in the darkest depths of the forest, three men dressed in army green camouflage sat next to a small fire. The firelight flickered across their sinister faces. They spoke in hushed tones as they ate their kill with dirty, unwashed hands. They completed their tasks of making snares: snares that would trap tiny fingers of baby gorillas. They would capture their quarry in the early morning.

The Wildlife Divas could not have arrived at a better time.

CHAPTER 8

A FRIGHTFUL NIGHT

Storm was the first to wake up, feeling excited about the day ahead. Shortly after breakfast, they were heading into the jungle. She counted three fingers, making sure she had memorized rules one, two, and three. She yawned, stretched, and did a sleepy butt scratch as she prepared to get out of bed. She had one foot on the floor when she noticed an awful noise.

She followed the sound as her eyes scanned the bed. Four distinct lumps lay beneath the covers. One with arms flung wildly, her body hanging half-on and half-off the bed, mouth wide open, was Ebony. She was snoring loudly. Storm wrinkled her nose and waved her hand back and forth.

"Pheew. Mouthwash," she said, wondering how the entire crew ended up in bed with her and Cherie.

Last night as everyone went to their sleeping quarters, the geeky tech girls, Kyloni and Valerie, were assigned a room together. They walked away discussing the latest in computer technology, video footage that needed editing, and algorithms that would make their videos go viral on their social media pages.

Ebony and Yalani would share a room, their conversation covering the latest hair styles, makeup tips, clothing trends, and what they would wear tomorrow, while Storm would room with Cherie to be kept out of trouble. *But how did everyone end up in their room?*

* * *

Several hours before her alarm clock went off, Yalani awoke, startled from a deep slumber. In pitch-black darkness, she thought she'd heard a noise. She strained her ears, listening carefully for several seconds. Nothing. Maybe she was dreaming. She lay back, snuggled under the blanket, and closed her eyes again.

Her eyes flew open wide. There it was again. This time there was no mistaking the snarling of some sort of beasts just outside their window.

"Oh no. Oh my gosh!" Her panic rising, Yalani quickly pulled the covers over her head, trembling. "Ebony!" she whispered, frightened.

Ebony responded with a muffled grunt, turned over, and started to snore again. The snarling continued, louder and closer this time.

She called again, "Ebony, wake up, I think there's something outside our window. Ebony!"

"Huh. What? Oh my god, what's the matter now?" was her grumpy response until she too heard the growls and snarls of the creatures. She sat up like a bolt of lightning, tearing off her sleep mask. "What was that?" She asked, now just as scared as her roommate.

Ebony grabbed the flashlight on the nightstand between their beds and switched it on. Yellow light lit up the room, casting a shadow upon the window. And to their horror, the outline of the animals could be seen, something with a hunched back and long tail. And when the beasts opened their mouths, very large teeth could be seen, like a large attack dog.

There were two of them. They bumped into the side of the wall just beneath their window. Yalani screamed. Throwing off the covers, she launched herself out of bed, sprinting toward the bedroom door with Ebony close on her heels. They tumbled through the door, roughly landing in a heap atop one another on the floor, momentarily dazed.

Kyloni and Valerie, hearing the commotion, exited their bedroom. They'd heard the noises too and were already out of bed to investigate when they heard the scream and loud crash.

"What happened? Are you guys okay?" Valerie whispered, lending a hand to help Yalani from the floor.

"Oh no. Oh my gosh. There was something in our room trying to attack us." Yalani exaggerated.

"That is a near impossibility. I personally made sure all doors were locked and windows tightly shut when we went to bed. Nothing could have gotten in here." Kyloni explained as she reached out to help Ebony.

"Well, maybe not in our room exactly, but it was definitely scratching at our window attempting to get in," Yalani admitted, her face contorted into a rat-like expression as she imitated an animal digging a hole. "Right, Ebony?"

"No doubt. There was something at our window. Did you hear it too?" Ebony's voice was edged with fear.

"Yes, we did. I've never heard anything like that before in my entire life. I must say, I am curious as to what species of animal it could be. Possibly a *Civettictis Civetta,* commonly known as the Civet Cat. Oh, or maybe a *Ugandan*

Red Colobus monkey. They're both nocturnal animals." Kyloni started walking toward the door leading outside their sleeping quarters, curiosity getting the best of her.

"Where do you think you're going?" Ebony asked.

"I'd like to see what's out there."

"Are you out of your mind? Don't you dare open that door!" Ebony warned in a screaming whisper.

"Relax. I'm just going to take a quick peek outside." Kyloni placed her hand on the doorknob and turned it slowly. Inch by inch, the door creaked open, making a creepy haunted house sound.

They all huddled closely behind her peeking over her shoulder. Yalani stood in the rear, biting her nails.

"Oh no. Oh my gosh," she whimpered.

"Flashlight." Kyloni ordered. Ebony passed it forward. A narrow beam of light shot across the darkness just in time to catch two beastly figures the size of pit bulls disappearing into the bushes thrashing, growling, and snarling.

They hadn't noticed Miss Cherie as she quietly walked up behind the group. She tapped Yalani on the shoulder and asked, "What are you all doing out of bed?"

A chorus of screams erupted, enough to wake every member of the camp as well as every living creature in the forest. Even normally cool, collected Kyloni screamed and tossed the flashlight into the air, slamming the door shut. This night, there was no convincing any of them to go back to their bedrooms. Yalani pleaded with sad, solemn puppy dog eyes.

"Can we pretty pleeease stay with you tonight? I don't want to sleep in there. Those things almost came through our window!" Yalani said, exaggerating.

The others chimed in, "Just for tonight!" Although Miss Cherie managed to calm their fears, they agreed on sleeping together tonight for safety's sake. Tomorrow everyone would remain in their own sleeping quarters no matter what happened.

They settled down, squeezing in tightly, six in one bed. Storm had slept through it all.

* * *

"Rise and shine!" Storm shouted, as she jumped up and down on the bed. Cherie, Ebony, Kyloni, Valerie, and Yalani groaned into their pillows.

They were awake now. Soon the group would start their first long day of hiking to find the band of gorillas. They hurried to the dining area for breakfast.

On the table their breakfast awaited. It was *Katogo*, the national dish of Uganda, the cook explained. The main ingredients were *matoke*, or green bananas, Irish potatoes, beef or chicken, tomatoes, and onions, making it a hearty, delicious stew. It was especially good for keeping away hunger while hiking and would keep their bellies full until lunch.

Storm especially loved it as she shoveled spoonful after spoonful into her mouth, chewing noisily. She declared how delicious the *katogo* was and how they too should try it because they didn't know what they were missing. Vegetarians Kyloni and Valerie chose to stick with the vegetarian dishes they were offered, which were so fresh that some of the foods were taken directly from the trees and gardens and swiftly prepared. After their tasty meal, it was time to go.

They were each assigned an individual guide to help them along the way. The hillsides and thick vegetation could be difficult to navigate.

With their help, they slid their arms through the straps of their packs and onto their backs, adjusting to the weight. Rain gear, a change of clothes, extra socks, pajamas, and other odds and ends were neatly packed. It could be several days before they returned to the campsite.

"Are we ready?" Kevin asked. Every one of them nodded yes in response, feeling both a bit of fear and excitement at what lay ahead.

Single file, they followed Kevin and their guides along the path leading into the rain forest, the sun slowly disappearing as foliage grew thicker. A bombardment of loud noises assaulted them. Birds sang their songs, frogs croaked, crickets chirped. They stopped to see a group of three baboons enjoying a breakfast of insects and ripened fruit. Several small monkeys saw them approaching and chattered in warning.

They looked around them and gave a backward glance. The camp that was in sight just moments ago had disappeared behind a wall of thick green vegetation. Huge leaves the size of elephant ears, giant ferns, and tree trunks, were as wide as cars. Vines, ropelike in thickness, hung from trees. It was as if the forest had swallowed them up in one huge gulp.

Then a strange and unexpected thing happened. In almost the same exact moment, birds and beasts alike stopped their songs and suddenly the forest fell silent.

CHAPTER 9

GORILLA TREKKING DAY ONE

The silence felt eerily unnatural and a little frightening. One minute the animals were playing a symphony of forest songs and the next moment, nothing. What could have possibly happened to all the animals?

Valerie, usually distracted with her face buried in the video camera, stopped in her tracks.

"Whoa!" she whispered, looking upward into the treetops, her video camera still recording.

"Kevin, where did all the animals go?" Storm turned in a complete circle, a puzzled look upon her face. She liked the sounds the animals made.

"Don't worry, this is perfectly normal." Kevin explained. "It's called 'anti-prey adaptation.'"

"A-dap-ta-tion?" Storm pronounced the word carefully. "What does that mean?" She asked curiously.

"Yes, anti-prey adaptation. An adaptation is a special skill—" Kevin began, but before he could finish his answer, Kyloni with her gigabyte storage of a brain answered instead. She pushed up her glasses from the tip of her nose with her middle finger.

"Adaptation is a special skill, as in the physical and behavioral abilities of an organism to better increase its chances of survival in its habitat and surrounding environment," she finished, pleased with her explanation.

"You're absolutely correct, Kyloni," Kevin confirmed. "Adaptation helps animals survive. To be 'anti-prey' means they hide themselves to keep from being eaten by other animals. Those things that are trying to eat them are called 'predators.' For example, some animals can change colors, so they blend in with their surroundings. It makes it difficult for predators to see them. Some animals have adapted to only coming out at night. This way they avoid predators while others remain high above in the trees. Then there are those who simply stop making noise until danger passes. They don't know if we are friendly or if we are coming to eat them."

"Ew, I like bugs, but I don't want to eat them." Storm made a yuck face.

Kevin chuckled. "Storm, I promise you, the bugs don't want to be eaten. So, you see, even a small amount of noise frightens them away. This is why the rules are so important," he said. After finishing this lesson, Kevin encouraged them to "get moving."

As they made their way along the path, the animals, sensing no danger, began their songs again. They looked around in wide-eyed wonder. The rain forest was nothing like the landscaped parks of neatly trimmed trees and beds of brightly colored flowers, or the hilly streets of their hometown of San Francisco. There was no Golden Gate Bridge. No crowds of tourist from all over the world visiting Fisherman's Wharf by the busloads. No sea lions at Pier 39 sunbathing, taking a rest from the frigid waters of the Pacific Ocean.

Kevin listened as the girls talked. He'd never been to San Francisco.

"I would like to visit one day. It sounds interesting and beautiful."

"Yes Kevin, you should come and visit us one day. We'll take you on a grand tour of our city." Cherie said, offering an open invitation. "It would be an honor."

Kevin smiled, nodding in approval.

In the Bwindi Impenetrable Forest, there were 350 different species of birds. Their guides offered these and other facts as they hiked. The Divas watched, delighted, using binoculars to view them flying from tree limbs to treetops, colored as brightly as the kites they fly back home in Golden Gate Park's Crissy Field.

The Bluebill, just as its name suggests, has a blue bill and its head is a deep dark red, the color of roses. Then there was the African Emerald Cuckoo, its feathers a bright green that matched the green leaves and vines surrounding them and its brightly yellow underbelly, making them easily identifiable.

Kevin was enormously proud of his country.

"Here in the southwest of Uganda, we are known not only for our gorillas, but our tea plantations as well," he explained. "Oh, and let's not forget the *Pygmies*, which we call *Batwa* or *Forest People*. They have lived in the forest even before the gorillas arrived."

"*Ba-twa*," Ebony pronounced the word carefully. Yalani repeated the word after her.

Yalani asked, "Can we go meet the Batwa?"

"It may be possible," he replied. "Maybe when you return to visit Uganda, we can take a special trip to meet them."

She beamed, happy with the answer. She glanced at Ebony, who nodded her approval and gave her a thumbs up.

"This is also one of the oldest forests on the entire planet. It's twenty-five thousand years old and has one of the richest ecosystems in the world," Kevin said proudly. You could tell he'd told this story many times before and loved this part.

"In Bwindi, we have 120 species of mammals. We'll come across several of them, like the monkeys above us now." They peered into the treetops and watched as they traveled from limb to limb, never touching the ground. "We even have forest elephants."

"Elephants?" Storm asked, surprised. "How can elephants live here? There are so many trees and bushes. They have no room to walk around."

"You'd be surprised at how well they manage to live here. They are mysterious, surprisingly quiet, and it's true they are rarely seen, but they are here. The trees and giant leaves are a perfect hiding place. Elephants are *herbivores*. You know what that means, right? It means they only eat roots, grasses, fruit, leaves, and vegetables. There's plenty of food—" Kyloni interrupted, pushing up her glasses.

"Now this of course would exclude insects, spiders, and a few other animals, like dogs and cats, as they all eat flesh of other animals. Herbivores only eat things that require photosynthesis to live." Her nimble mind, filled with facts about many subjects.

"You are correct again, Kyloni. Herbivores do not eat meat." Continuing his lesson, he added, "We also have two hundred species of trees. Storm, I know you'll like this fact: there are over two hundred species of butterflies."

As if on cue, several Cream-banded Swallowtail butterflies and several other species flittered and took flight from the ground as they passed by. They'd found something extremely tasty to eat. Most likely salt. They laughed as Storm leapt in the air, chasing butterflies in all directions.

Onward they trekked deeper into the rainforest. It was a difficult, uphill climb. The vines on the forest floor snagged and tangled around their hiking boots, tripping them. Their guides helped them keep their balance, for they all had difficulty in this jungle terrain.

For nearly two hours they searched. Still no gorillas in sight.

They came upon a nesting sight, a place where the gorillas made their beds and slept for the night. This was a good sign. Another good sign was gorilla poop. According to Kevin, the poop was less than twenty-four hours old. This meant the gorillas could be anywhere in the forest with them. They had to be nearby. The team continued to climb, encouraged by their find.

By hour three, it began to rain. Hard! Thunder could be heard above the tree canopy and lighting flashed all around them. This was becoming a nightmare. Add pouring rain with walking uphill, vines snagging on their feet, and branches in their faces and tangling their hair. Now everything was wet and slippery, their boots sucked down by thick mud. It was like walking through gooey slime. They were all caught up in their own miserable thoughts when suddenly Kevin held up a hand, signaling them to stop. They froze in their steps.

He whispered quietly, "Look there, to your left. Do you see him?"

They stretched and craned their necks for a better look. Hidden in plain sight, nearly directly in their path, stood a magnificent beast—a male elephant. He paid no attention to them as he enjoyed his breakfast, stripping long pieces of tree bark with the nimble tip of his trunk. As if on cue the rain stopped.

Valerie walked up to the front of the group and stood next to Kevin. She tapped the record button and watched in wonderment. Slowly creeping forward, their footsteps as quiet as walking on cotton, they listened carefully to Kevin's instructions.

"Quiet. We don't want to disturb him. We are so incredibly lucky to see him. Finding a forest elephant rarely happens. They are such shy creatures. I think we will name him *Bahati*, which means 'luck.' This elephant is quite old, probably in his forties or fifties judging by the size of his tusks. He is truly lucky to have lived so long. Poachers also hunt elephants. They would kill an entire elephant for his ivory tusks," Kevin explained.

They watched in silence as the ancient pachyderm devoured giant leaves as well as tree bark. The rain stopped. The newly arriving sun shone brightly through the small clearing. Puffs of steam rose off the back of the giant beast, his body heat mixing with the cool mountain air and sunshine. He finished eating, took two steps backward, and disappeared like magic into the lush green forest just as suddenly as he appeared.

They let out a collective sigh. What a beautiful, majestic animal. Onward they trekked.

"Are we there yet?" Storm asked again for the tenth time.

Ebony rolled her eyes, mimicking her words silently.

"Are we there yet? What a brat!" she muttered under her breath.

Storm responded by sticking out her tongue and saying one word. "*Nabbubi!*"

This sent Ebony scampering away to the opposite side of the group, as far away from Storm as possible! She did not want another spider incident!

They'd been hiking for hours now. Everyone was growing tired, their backpacks were getting heavier with every step, and still they had not seen any gorillas or poachers. Only more gorilla poop! It was beginning to look as if they were there for no reason at all.

"Kevin, can you give us a few facts about gorillas? Do gorillas live alone?" Kyloni asked, trying to keep everyone interested and involved, instead of concentrating on the misery of being wet and not finding the gorillas.

Kevin was happy to explain. "There are times when we do not find gorilla families immediately. Every day they move to a different location to find food and water."

"Families? A different location?" Yalani questioned.

"Yes, families, and to answer your question, gorillas do not live alone," Kevin continued, "just like you and your family. There are the mothers and babies, brothers and sisters, aunts and uncles, and the Silverback."

"A Silverback?" Storm interrupted him. "Why do they call him a Silverback? Is he like a football quarterback like Jimmy Garoppolo? He's the quarterback for our favorite team, the San Francisco Forty-Niners. Ga-rop-po-lo, Ga-rop-po-lo!" She did her famous "happy dance," skipping around excitedly.

"No," Kevin chuckled. "Nothing like a football quarterback, you cheeky little thing." He reached over and tweaked Storm's nose and she giggled.

"The Silverback is the head of the family. He protects them from danger, just as a human father would when he grows up and becomes a man," he teased, beating his chest, making a growling sound deep in his chest, just as a gorilla would.

"Which is around the age of thirteen," he continued, "a streak of silver appears across the middle of his back. The Silverback decides what the family will do for the day. For example, where they will eat, which river they will drink from, and where they will sleep at night."

"Where do gorillas sleep?" Valerie whispered as her head popped up from behind her camera. This was more than anyone had heard her speak in some time.

"Anywhere he wants," Kevin said with a laugh. "Silverbacks can weigh up to 270 kilograms."

Forgetting rule number three, Storm screeched.

"*270 kilos!* Did he just say..." she turned and looked at Cherie and then back at Kevin. "Did you just say 270 kilograms!"

"Storm, lower your voice." Cheri scolded. "Not so loud you're scaring the animals and probably the gorillas too, if there are any nearby." She looked up into the trees to see several leaves falling to the ground where animals had scurried at the sound of her voice.

"Oh, sorry!" Storm tried to whisper. "But Cheri, he said 270 kilograms," she said, pointing her finger at Kevin, who could not contain the smile on his face. She calculated the equation. "1 kilogram is equal to 2.2 pounds, multiply that by 270 kilograms, and that equals ..." Her eyes flew open wide in disbelief. She nearly shouted again! "That's 594 pounds rounded up to the nearest hundred that's—that's 600 pounds, Cherie! 600 pounds. Really?" She held up six fingers, this time whispering the number of fingers she held up. "*Six!*"

They stared, their mouths gaped wide open in astonishment! How does she do that? How is it humanly possible to calculate those numbers in her head so fast and without the help of a calculator!

"What?" Storm asked, confused by all the attention. "Why are you staring at me? What'd I do this time?" She was prepared for another scolding.

"You are amazing, simply amazing. Your math skills are just out of this world!" Miss Cherie pulled her close and hugged her. Storm beamed with pride, relieved she was not in trouble again.

They continued their trek deeper in the rainforest. Higher and higher they climbed into the green-covered hillsides, their guides holding their hands occasionally as they slipped on wet grasses and slick rocks. The other guides chopped away leaves, clearing a path in front of them. Six hours of hiking in the rainforest, chopping, climbing, swatting away bugs, a steady drizzle of rain, and still no gorillas.

* * *

So distracted they were by the miserable conditions, no one noticed the three men quickly scurrying from the path moments before they came around the bend. Blending in with their surroundings, they crouched low, perfectly hidden.

They watched, frozen in place as Kevin, the guides, and the Wildlife Divas passed, unaware of their presence. As the last guide moved past, they grabbed two brown bags and quickly sprinted off in the opposite direction. Weak, frightened whines and whimpers could be heard from the bags as the poachers ran deeper into the forest, disappearing into the night.

* * *

Reaching camp, they dropped their heavy water-logged backpacks, removed their raincoats, wet shoes, and socks, and hung them up to dry. There was no celebration this evening. They ate their meals quietly, faces set in grim disappointment. Cherie feared at this rate they would not complete their mission. She sighed, dismayed, but kept her thoughts to herself as not to discourage them. Tomorrow. Tomorrow had to be better.

CHAPTER 10

CRACK!

After the long, exhausting trek of rain and pure misery, the team were not in the cheeriest of moods. Most disappointing of all was not finding any signs of the gorillas, their main reason for being there. They ate dinner quietly, each deep in her own thoughts.

They had an early start in the morning, so immediately after dinner, they prepared themselves for bed. Away they went, paired as they had been the night before—Ebony and Yalani, Valerie and Kyloni, and Cherie and Storm—to their separate rooms.

It was Valerie, not Storm, who was the first to wake this morning. She giggled as she looked around the bedroom realizing that it happened again. They all ended up in the same bed with Cherie and Storm. One by one they'd crept into the room, not waiting for anything terrifying in the night to scare them.

Valerie caught Ebony in the middle of a morning stretch, her hair—as always—neatly braided and tied with a bandana scarf. But man, oh man, she made the ugliest faces ever when she yawned. And Valerie had gotten it all on video. Yes! She would use this video recording later! Valerie giggled.

"Good morning. *Wasuze otya*," she said cheerfully and was met with an evil glare.

"There is no sunshine. Get away from me," Ebony grumbled, pulling the covers up over her head, which only made Valerie laugh even harder. "*Wasuze otya*! Good morning! Time to rise and shine. Today is the day!" Valerie predicted as she recorded each and every one of their faces.

Cherie squeezed her eyes shut tightly against the bright lights of the iPhone in the dark room. "Valerie, please!" she protested. "Can we do this later when I'm awake completely?"

Valerie answered with a giggle and moved on to Yalani, who was in mid-nose scratch and making a honking noise that sounded very much like a goose!

"Oh, no you don't! Erase that!" Yalani shrieked. "Valerie, you *can't!* No!"

Again, she laughed, promising to edit that part out.

"Thank you!" Yalani said, clearly relieved.

"But can you do one thing for me? Can you make that sound again?" Ducking out of the way, she laughed as Yalani tossed a pillow at her in answer. She moved on to Storm.

"Storm," she cooed. "Wake *up!*" She tickled beneath her chin. Nothing. She took Storm's arm, lifting it high, shaking it, and then releasing it. It was like holding the arm of a rag doll.

"Stoooorm," she repeated, this time rocking her back and forth gently. Storm, in a deep, deep sleep sprawled across the bed, could not be moved. Valerie clapped her hands next to her ear. Nothing! She didn't move a muscle.

Incredible! How she sleeps so deeply is beyond imagination. It was like trying to wake a sleeping zombie. Valerie decided to leave Storm to sleep a little longer.

"Well ladies," Valerie said in her soft voice, sliding her iPhone into her jacket pocket. "It's time to get dressed and get back to the rain forest to find those gorillas."

At the word "*gorillas,*" Storm bolted upright out of her deep, coma-like sleep.

"Gorillas?" she shouted. She jumped out of bed, scrambling into her clothes. Hopping on one leg, she stumbled to the floor as she pulled on her pants and was dressed in an instant.

"I'm okay! That didn't hurt. I'm good. Okay, let's go!" They all laughed, watching as she hurriedly pulled on socks and hiking boots.

The team was now dressed and ready to go. They enjoyed a light breakfast of porridge, a dish very much like oatmeal, with fresh pineapple, bananas, and more katogo. Storm spooned in a mouthful and chewed happily, proclaiming it her most favorite dish in all of Uganda. They were on their way again in the early morning just as the sun began to rise.

As a reminder, Kevin quizzed them. "What's the first and most important rule, ladies?"

He cupped his hand to his ear waiting to hear their response.

They all said in unison, "Don't run?"

Kevin nodded his approval. "Right, off we go then. Let's find those gorillas!" Single file, they left the dense, green bush ahead of them.

They kept hiking higher and higher into the mountains through thickening trees and crawling vines that clawed at their clothing and tangled in their hair. Their guides chopped at thick vegetation to clear their path. Their boots were soaking wet after crossing a small stream in the forest. A stream of water which was a fresh water supply for the gorillas. They would not be too far away.

Kevin told them that on most occasions, they would find the gorillas within a day. In fact, more often they would spot them within hours. To go more than a day without finding them was highly unusual. Something was not quite right.

The sun was halfway across the African sky. As they came upon a clearing in the forest where trees were few, Kevin called a break. Here they would rest, eat lunch, and come up with a plan to locate the gorillas. They were free to roam wherever they wished, but this was not a zoo.

Each sighed with relief as they slid off their backpacks, dropping them to the ground with a thud. Their shoulders ached from the weight of the packs, which seem to have grown heavier with every kilometer.

Lunch was cheese and tomato sandwiches, along with a banana, hard-boiled egg, boxed mango juice, and water. The key was to keep hydrated by drinking plenty of water. Their guides, Simon and Seezi, sat alongside them talking about their futures and how one day how they would like to visit the United States of America, especially California.

Storm ate quickly, gobbling down her sandwich and mango juice. She had seen something and wanted to investigate. Dressed in her safari hat and jacket, she reached into a pocket and pulled out her magnifying glass. Looking through the pair of binoculars hanging around her neck, she looked for the object of curiosity.

There it was: a lizard with scaly skin and eyes that couldn't seem to focus as each eye looked in different directions. It was a chameleon! It was just a baby, so she wasn't afraid. Storm stuck out her finger as he slowly climbed from a branch onto the finger she held out. Its colors morphed from bright green which matched the leaves on the branch to a speckled brown color which matched her finger. Storm giggled. After examining the lizard, she placed him back on the tree branch where she'd found him.

Yalani and Ebony finished their lunches and found a grassy spot where they laid back to relax and watch monkeys play among the treetops. This place was peaceful and beautiful, a relief from the thick vines and undergrowth of the rainforest.

Since they were having such difficulty in locating the gorillas, Kevin sent trackers ahead to scout out their location. They soon returned with worried looks upon their faces. Moving away from the group for more privacy, they talked in excited whispers. What they had found was not a good sign.

They had come across the poacher's campsite. It was obvious that they left only moments before. Their campfire still burned, and their tools of torture were left behind. Most likely they heard the Divas coming and made their escape.

The scouts also found snares: traps used to capture gorillas. Babies especially were known to get fingers trapped and were unable to free themselves. The guides explained that even some adult gorillas had been caught in these cruel devices.

As Kevin spoke with the trackers in private, Valerie and Kyloni put their heads together to come up with their own plan. They had just the thing to help locate the gorillas: a drone.

As soon as they put on their safety glasses, Valerie and Kyloni began the pre-flight check. Battery properly charged? Check. Wings and camera? Check. And lastly, they made sure there was no debris clogging the engine. The drone beeped as a green light appeared when they pressed the "on" button.

Finding a flat surface on the ground, Valerie sat the drone there preparing for takeoff. Connecting the drone to her iPhone, Valerie calibrated the drone's compass by picking it up and turning in a 360-degree circle, then placing it back on the ground again. Kyloni held the controller and verified when it was complete. With all prechecks done, it was time to fly.

Valerie switched to "takeoff" mode, the engines whirred to life lifting the drone several feet from the ground.

"Did you remember to tap the 'return home' icon?" Kyloni asked. Valerie nodded yes without breaking concentration. Off the drone went in search of the gorillas.

The drone proved to be more difficult to fly under these circumstances. The forest vegetation was thick and nearly impassable in some places, but Valerie was able to carefully navigate the drone. She swerved several times, nearly crashing twice before finding a clearing where the drone could gain altitude.

Kyloni monitored the drone's video, even ducking when the drone nearly crashed into a tree although she was in no danger.

Something whirred past the drone, nearly hitting it.

"What was that?" Kyloni asked. She peered closely at the monitor screen. "Did you see it? I think someone threw an object at our drone!"

Voices, three distinct male voices, talked excitedly. Someone threw another object that nearly clipped a propeller.

"Whoa, that was close!" Kyloni warned. The drone hovered above the men, recording their actions. They gestured wildly at the drone. This time one of them threw a stick.

Valerie pushed the controller up and to the left, making the drone maneuver out of the way just in the nick of time.

"Valerie," Kyloni warned, eyes growing wide with shock and disbelief. "He's got a gun." As her brain registered this fact, her voice became more urgent. "He's got a gun! He's aiming at our drone!" She screamed. "Get outta there *now!* Home base, home base! Bring it back to home base!"

Crack! The sound of the rifle shot split the air. The drone lurched as it tried to make its escape. Grim faced and determined, Valerie activated the "return home" button. She bit her bottom lip as she willed the drone to gain altitude as it sputtered and struggled. The gunshot had shattered one of its engines. Yet the drone continued to climb higher. *Crack!* A second shot rang out.

The trackers were in a deep conversation with Kevin when the first shot rang out. They looked at one another in alarmed surprise. Readying their own rifles, they were already running full speed into the rainforest when the second shot rang out.

CHAPTER 11

POACHERS, GORILLAS, AND BABIES, OH MY!

Kyloni's screams sent Cherie racing across the field toward them. Her protective instincts kicking in, she grabbed Storm by the arm, pulling her along with her. The sound of the rifle shot made every single member of the gorilla trekking team duck and hide for cover. The girls were familiar with the sound of gunfire from their own San Francisco neighborhood and practiced this exercise along with earthquake drills on a monthly basis. Huddled together, they watched as Kevin and the trackers with their machine guns strapped across their backs raced armed and unafraid into the forest.

Cherie, always the protector, made sure everyone was okay, including their guides. Each one of them was unharmed.

Dropping from the sky, the injured drone crashed exactly in the place on the ground where it started—home base. Valerie and Kyloni examined it. Out of frustration, Kyloni threw it to the ground. It was ruined; there was no saving it.

Valerie picked it back up. All was not lost. She could save the video, she explained to Kyloni. She uploaded the camera feed to the iCloud where it would be stored permanently.

The guides and the Wildlife Divas took turns examining the gunshot wound to the drone, passing it from one to another. They were so absorbed in the drone they did not hear the forthcoming danger barreling through the jungle. And it was coming their way.

There was a rumble coming from the forest. It started as a faint sound and was now growing louder. Sounds of boots crunching, tree branches snapping.

The first warning was birds suddenly taking flight. They watched a mated pair of Great Blue Turacos covered in blue feathers and green feathered underbellies fly away. Beautiful birds with yellow beaks with red tips that looked like lipstick had been applied took to the skies in escape.

Storm and Yalani saw the beautiful creatures take flight and were awed by their beauty. Next came Tree Hyraxes, small furry mammals that looked like the cross between a bunny and a cat with sharp, feline teeth. They shrieked in terror as they ran by. A mother forest hog with several babies with rough, black fur and sharp, curved tusks came dashing past Yalani in the same fashion, all shrieks and ear-splitting squeals, and they rushed past. Yalani turned to watching them go as she held up one hand, shading her eyes. What could have gotten into these animals and why were they so frightened? There are three natural reactions most animals and humans have when faced with danger: fighting, fleeing, or freezing in place.

They could then hear several angry men shouting as they ran through the forest. It was the sound of combat boots trampling the ground, shaking the earth. It is what sent all the creatures big and small fleeing for their lives.

Three men all dressed in black were the first to burst through the dense forest. Giving chase to those three were members of the Ugandan Wildlife Authority with their weapons drawn. Behind them were Kevin and the trackers who'd run into the forest after hearing the gunshots ring out.

Hearing the commotion, Yalani whirled around to come face to face with the three fleeing poachers. There was no time to fight nor to flee. She instead froze in place, wide-eyed and filled with terror. Her mouth opened to scream, but it was too late. She could only brace herself for impact.

And impact they did. She held out her hands, closed her eyes, and turned her head aside as if it would stop the collision from happening. The men's faces were a mask of surprise when—*boom*—the first man ran into her head on. The second and third men, only steps behind him, were each carrying a brown sack with a thick cord wrapped around the top. They tumbled over them, the two sacks flying and somersaulting through the air. The two poachers scrambled swiftly to their feet in an attempt to get away. As Kevin and the trackers arrived, they saw the men and set off after them. They tackled one man and the other from behind.

Kevin, Jimbo, and Cherie rushed over to help Yalani up from the ground, removing debris from her hair and clothing. The UWA soldiers held all three poachers to the ground, handcuffing them and placing them under arrest. The poachers were captured!

Cherie, the guides, and Ebony all ran in the direction toward their fallen Diva. Ebony leapt into the air like a seasoned athlete. Her outstretched hands caught both sacks midair as she tumbled, rolled, and landed sprawled in a nearby bush with both brown sacks tucked protectively in her arms. She'd saved them. And Yalani had stopped them!

Every poacher's nightmare was being caught for the crime of poaching. The Ugandan Wildlife Authority penalties were considerable. And for this crime, they would pay dearly. Crimes of this nature could have them jailed for many years. Some as much as seventy-five years, depending upon the nature of the crimes. They were caught red-handed. The UWA officers were upon them. The chase left them breathing heavily, out of breath.

They were surprised by what happened. How had this brave young girl stood in front of the poachers, blocking their way, and stopping them from getting away with their crime? If not for her courage, they would have surely gotten away. Her bravery would be celebrated later.

Yalani was in a daze, her head spinning dizzily. "Oh no. Oh my gosh! W-w-what happened?" Everything happened so fast! One minute she was standing there watching the three men running toward her, her hands outstretched, and the next moment she was being helped from the ground.

Rushing to her aid were Cherie, her guide Jimbo, and Kevin.

"Are you alright? Are you hurt?" Kevin asked her, his questions urgent and concerned.

"I—I—I think I'm okay ..." Yalani responded, not sure if she was really okay or not. "What happened?" she asked again, placing her hand upon her forehead to stop the spinning.

Cherie was a nervous wreck, pacing back and forth. These girls were her responsibility; she would do anything to keep them from harm. It was her duty to get the girls home safely. This could have turned out to be a disaster, she thought to herself.

"Yalani, please tell me you're okay?" Cherie asked anxiously.

"Yes, Cherie, I'm okay. I'm not hurt. I was just a little dizzy, but I'm okay now!" Yalani assured her. Well ... Maybe her pride was a little hurt. Her face flamed red in embarrassment. She began to cry.

"I'm really sorry Cherie. Kevin, I'm sorry I let you down. Jimbo, I apologize, I said I would try to be braver. I wasn't trying to get in the way. I think I may have hurt those men," she finished the sentence in a murmur, hanging her head in shame.

"You brilliant, brilliant girl, you have no idea what you've done, do you?" Kevin grabbed her by both shoulders in amazement of what she'd accomplished. "You stopped the poachers dead in their tracks, and I'm quite sure you've saved a couple of baby gorillas as well!"

"Who? Who me?" Yalani asked, completely flabbergasted, "Poachers? Baby gorillas? I—I saved them?" she asked in disbelief.

She looked at each of their faces. It was not disappointment she saw; it was pride. They were proud of her! The smiles upon their faces proved it.

Now that they were certain Yalani was okay, Kyloni, Valerie, and Storm rushed to Ebony's side.

"Oh my goodness! Are you okay?" Kyloni asked. She was afraid Ebony injured herself when she tumbled and landed on top of the bush.

"Ebony! That was a wicked cool catch!" Storm said as she danced about excitedly. "It was like Jimmy Garoppolo throwing a pass for a touchdown! Woo! Touchdown!"

Storm shouted excitedly as she demonstrated Ebony leaping through the air. "It was great!"

Kyloni interrupted. She needed Storm to focus her attention on what they were doing. "Storm, help me! Grab her arm so we can lift her! Remember the rules," she reminded her.

"Oh … Yes, I'm sorry, Kyloni! Ebony, are you all right?" Storm questioned. Sometimes her excitement got the best of her. They helped her sit up slowly along with the help of their guides, Seezi and Emmanuel.

The two brown sacks were still tucked protectively in Ebony's arms. There was movement inside. At first a little squirming, then thrashing around the bag, trying to escape. Muffled, whimpering cries were coming from both. It was the kidnapped gorilla babies.

Ebony could feel the warmth of their bodies through the sacks and their little fingers grasping at her.

"Shh, quiet babies," Ebony cooed and rocked them as a mother would have done.

She was about to open one of the cloth sacks as Kevin, Cherie, and Yalani walked over. Kevin's shout stopped her immediately.

"No Ebony! *Stop*! Don't open that bag!" Kevin shouted, breaking his own rule number two.

CHAPTER 12

DNA

Ebony's heart nearly jumped out of her chest, frightened. Kevin ran toward her full speed, waving his arms and shouting. For their entire trip he had been pleasant and fun with never an angry word.

Confused by his anger, Ebony pulled back, an automatic reflex of fear and protectiveness. She used her body to shield and protect the bags as the squirming and whimpering continued inside.

She crouched down, gently setting both bags on the ground. She cooed, attempting to quiet them. She turned and stood full height, willing to combat anyone to protect these babies.

"I was only going to open the bags a little. I wanted to make sure they're okay," she explained, concerned about their safety. "Don't you hear them crying? And they need fresh air."

Kevin could hear them and was just as anxious to let them out of the sacks. He wanted the same thing: to make sure they were unharmed. But this important step could not be missed. It was not only for the safety and protection of the babies, but the entire population of gorillas in the Bwindi Impenetrable Forest.

He needed to explain what they were not fully aware of. The greatest threats to mountain gorillas, besides the loss of habitat and poaching, was *human diseases.*

"Ebony, relax. I apologize. I didn't mean to scare you." He noticed her balled fists and fighting stance. "Allow me to explain. I shouted at you but not out of anger. Again, I apologize. The bags need to remain closed until we can put on proper protection. They have been exposed to possible diseases and infections because of the poachers. They don't care about these animals. We must always use medical masks and gloves when handling them. Not for our sake, but for their health and safety. These great apes are one of the closest related to human beings like you and I. They share 98.3 percent of the same DNA as we do."

"Are you saying that we humans are that closely related to mountain gorillas? Our genetic sequencing is only 1.7 percent different from theirs?" Cherie asked. This was mind boggling. She had no idea we were so closely related to this animal species. Curiously, she continued. "What other human qualities do they share with us?"

"Well, let's see," Kevin folded his arms across his chest. Tapping a finger on his chin as he thought. "They can and have in the past become infected with human diseases such as measles, the flu, even upper respiratory infections, like pneumonia. It's especially important now with the coronavirus epidemic to wear protective gear." He could not stress the importance of protecting the health of the gorillas. He added, "And if left untreated, these diseases can spread throughout an entire gorilla community. And if not caught in time, it can have the same effect as it does with us."

Ebony nodded in understanding. She would do anything to help protect these babies.

"For humans, it's easy. We go to the doctor's office and have an exam. If we're sick, we're given a prescription for medication and we're out of the doctor's office in thirty minutes. This is not true for gorillas."

Ebony nodded. What Kevin explained was true.

Gathering closer to Kevin, each person received a new face mask and a pair of rubber gloves. Everyone wanted a closer look at the babies.

"Let's be as quiet as possible and stand back." Kevin cautioned. "We don't want to scare them.

They've been through enough already." They each gave the frightened babies a little extra space.

Storm stood on tiptoes, craning her neck up down and around trying to see the babies. Valerie and Kyloni pulled her forward to stand in front of them for a better view.

"I've already radioed ahead to the veterinarians for medical assistance. They will be here shortly. Before being released back to their families, they will need to be examined for injuries and given a clean bill of health. Hopefully, these evil poachers did not kill the families. It's happened in the past; whole families of gorillas are massacred just to make a profit."

Kevin's words reminded Kyloni about a similar situation in Rwanda. She'd researched and read about the world-famous Doctor Dian Fossey, the famous Primatologist, who gave her life protecting mountain gorillas.

Kevin turned and glared angrily at the poachers. They sat on the ground, hands handcuffed behind their backs. They were caught red-handed, the gorilla babies in their possession. The Ugandan Wildlife Authority without a doubt had the right men in custody. They were going to jail. UWA had a zero-tolerance policy for poachers. The men hung their heads in shame as everyone in their party—the trackers, the guides, and the Wildlife Divas team—turned to look at them.

He passed Ebony a pair of gloves and a mask. A protective instinct had kicked in; she refused to release the babies to anyone. Using her elbows to keep the opening of both bags against her body, she prevented the squirming babies from climbing out.

Ebony slipped on the mask, which looked like a doctor's surgical mask, then tried slipping on a rubber glove on her right hand with great difficulty. She needed both hands but did not want to release the bags. She felt oddly protective toward them, especially after hearing what they've had to live through in the hands of these terrible men.

"Here you go," Kevin offered, "let me help you with that." He stretched the glove open so she could slip her hand in with ease.

"Thank you, Kevin." A grateful smile accompanied Ebony's thank you.

She sat on the ground, the two sacks held firmly between her knees. Gently, she untied the rope on the first bag. The sack dropped to the ground, exposing a small, black ball of fur. A tiny pair of black hands reached up in the air, wanting to be picked up. While the backs of its hands were covered in fur, the baby's palms and fingers were a beautiful leather-like skin, black as obsidian stone.

She reached out both hands and waited. Ebony held her breath, afraid to make any sudden movement that might frighten the tiny creature. It raised its head. Deep, chocolate-brown eyes met hers. For a split second, Ebony was surprised and confused by what she saw.

The expression in the baby's eyes told the story. For its entire short life, it was always surrounded by family, being loved and protected. Then it was snatched away from its mother, kidnapped, roughly handled, and tossed into an old, dirty bag. Ebony could see the fear and trauma in its large, brown eyes as they locked with her own.

Valerie circled quietly, capturing the moment on video as the baby grasped her fingers and climbed into her arms, nuzzling its body against hers for warmth and safety.

She did the same with the second baby. Carefully, Ebony opened the second bag. The crying baby quickly crawled out of the sack before she could open it completely.

This baby wasn't as calm. It jumped out of the sack and jumped in Ebony's arms. The ordeal had taken a toll on the second baby. It was frightened and clung tightly, his face nearly buried under her jacket, shivering in fear. No one else could come near it without the baby making frightened whimpering sounds.

For Ebony and the team, it all finally made sense. They finally understood the true nature of their mission and purpose for their team. This was not just about fun trips and traveling. It was about saving the lives of critically endangered animals.

After several minutes, both babies calmed. They somehow sensed the love growing in Ebony's heart and how much she cared.

They were touching, grasping each other's hands, and grooming one another. Gorillas used grooming as a way of relaxing and calming each other.

They made little funny grunts and grumbling sounds which reassured each other they were safe.

They both explored Ebony, touching the buttons on her shirt and each taking turns grabbing and pulling her hair, touching her lips and nose. She sat with the silliest grin on her face they'd ever seen, transformed. The team looked on smiling at the tender moment and felt quite pleased with themselves. Thanks to Yalani, they'd saved these two babies from a terrible future.

CHAPTER 13

MISSION ACCOMPLISHED

——

Doctor Fred Nizeyimana, the gorilla doctor, arrived with his team, causing a buzz of excitement. He was one of the lead veterinarians and foremost experts on the health and wellness of mountain gorillas in Bwindi. Kevin and the doctor were well acquainted. While Kevin helped tourists gain Gorilla Trekking Permits to visit the gorillas, Dr. Fred helped maintain the health of several different gorilla family groups within Bwindi. Kevin introduced him to the team.

"Hey, Dr. Fred, nice seeing you again." Kevin welcomed him with a handshake and pat on the back. "I'd like you to meet the Wildlife Divas Adventure Team all the way from San Francisco, California. They are here on special assignment to help stop poachers from stealing our gorilla babies. And as you can see, we have been quite successful because of these young ladies and especially this one standing here next to me."

He motioned Yalani forward to meet Dr. Fred.

"Meet Yalani, who single handedly stopped those three miserable poachers red-handed. Yalani, this is Dr. Fred."

She moved forward shyly, reaching out a glove-covered hand to shake Dr. Fred's.

"It's a pleasure to meet you, Yalani. I cannot thank you enough for your bravery. I'm honored and hugely impressed."

"It's a pleasure to meet you too." Yalani was slightly embarrassed by all the attention.

"And this is Ebony," Kevin introduced her as he and Dr. Fred took a few steps to where she still sat, holding both babies in her arms. Noticing how they clung to Ebony as they would their own mother, Dr. Fred commented.

"Ah, Ebony, our substitute gorilla mama," he chuckled with a friendly smile. "It takes a special person to earn the trust of gorillas so quickly. It shows what a compassionate and loving soul you are." He praised characteristics that even she hadn't realized she had.

Ebony beamed with pride at the compliment. She was not used to being thought of as nice to others. She blushed and thanked Dr. Fred.

"May I?" He motioned toward the one resting comfortably in her left arm. Ebony nodded yes and passed the baby over to the Doctor. He of all people understood the bond of mothers and infants, humans and gorillas alike. It was true and natural for nearly all animal species to protect their young.

Dr. Fred examined the first baby for any physical injuries, checking it from head to toe. He took the stethoscope and placed the earbuds into his ears, listening to its heartbeat. The baby was in perfect health.

"The eyes are bright and clear, no physical injuries. He's hungry, but there's nothing the matter with him otherwise."

"He?" Ebony asked, smiling. "A little boy." She hugged him close.

"Yes, he is a boy." Dr. Fred handed baby number one back to Ebony and switched him for baby number two. "Hm, this little fellow is not so lucky." Dr. Fred listened to the baby's heartbeat. Baby number two was weak, warm with fever, and had a festering, infected wound around his wrist.

"Tsk tsk. This is not good. You see here," he pointed to the infected area, "this is how they captured him with a wire snare that cut into his skin." He turned the baby's arm to see that the bloody wound encircled his entire wrist.

Storm tugged on the sleeve of Dr. Fred. He knelt down to give her a closer look. "Does it hurt?" she asked.

"Dr. Fred, this is the youngest of the team, Storm," Kevin said and added, "Recording the video is Valerie." Valerie nodded as she continued to video Dr. Fred's examination of the baby's wound.

"Yes, Storm, I'm afraid so," he responded unhappily as he continued his examination.

His other team members were preparing to use a dart gun with a tranquilizer to put the wounded baby to sleep. One filled a syringe with a thick liquid and yet another prepared a vitamin solution for both babies to get them healthy and strong. After being captured, they were missing important vitamins and nutrients they would have gotten from their mother's milk.

Kyloni stood next to them, listening intently, typing out notes while watching what they were preparing to do next. Under Cherie's homeschooling education, she was entering her first year of college in the upcoming school year. She had been leaning toward becoming an Environmental Ecology Scientist, but maybe, just maybe, she may change her academic major to Animal Sciences so she can become a veterinarian like Dr. Fred. Or she could study to become a primatologist like Dr. Fossey, who was also from San Francisco. Before her death, Dr. Fossey worked with mountain gorillas in the Virunga Volcanic National Park in Rwanda. She even wrote a book which later became a movie titled *Gorillas in the Mist.*

"Dr. Fred, I'm Kyloni. It's a pleasure to meet you. Now, do my eyes deceive me or am I witnessing a single zygote which split into two embryos? Monozygotic. Is my observation correct, doctor?" she pushed up her glasses using an index finger, examining the baby as closely as the doctor.

Astonished, Dr. Fred replied, "Wow, that is a great observation. Kyloni, is it? Yes, you are correct. They are the exact same age. Notice their eyes and face shape are the same as well. These babies are genetically identical twins. I think you would be a wonderful addition to our team, Kyloni. Please give it some serious thought. I believe you would make an excellent veterinarian."

She beamed with pride, quite pleased with herself.

"Here, now pay close attention to how we dress the wound." He first cleaned the wound with a solution and applied an antibacterial ointment, followed by an injection that would keep the injury from becoming infected for weeks to come. It was a sort of boost to the immune system while his wound healed. Vitamins were given to both babies, who whimpered and scrambled back into Ebony's arms after their examination and treatment were completed.

* * *

They made their way through the forest. It had begun to rain heavily. A muddied path lay in front of them, one that had been used hundreds of times before. It led them out of the rainforest and back to the lodge where they spent the first night. All they needed to do now was return the babies to their family. The gorilla group would be near the silverback, so they were close.

The sun would be setting soon, and complete darkness would follow. Another night in the rainforest would not be a good idea with a group of dangerous poachers within the group. They occasionally turned to stare at the men, especially Yalani. No, they did not want to spend a minute longer than necessary.

There were times when these situations did now go well, especially when kidnapped infants could not be returned to their families. In the past poachers would wipe out entire members of a family just to steal the babies. Once considered an orphan, their lives would take a different path.

GRACE, the new Gorilla Rehabilitation and Conservation Education Center, located in the Democratic Republic of Congo, is a new, state-of-the-art facility. Sponsored by the Dian Fossey Gorilla Fund, it was important to the gorilla populations and would accept them from any country in need of their services. The hope was that one day they could return to the forest as a family.

Sometimes poachers get away with their dastardly deeds and successfully sell babies on the black market, receiving thousands of dollars for their awful trade. And sadder still is that mountain gorillas do not survive very long in captivity and not even in zoos. The girls felt that gorillas must be free to roam the forests with their families where they thrive.

* * *

Onward they marched, Kevin and Dr. Fred at the front of the group as they snaked through the trail, picking up the pace in order to reach base camp before dark. Ebony, carrying the twin boys, was behind them along with their guides, and in the rear were the wildlife authority with their powerful guns aimed at the three poachers, their hands tied behind their backs.

What happened next took them all by surprise. It would be difficult to describe later as it took place with astounding speed. The Silverback appeared out of nowhere from the thick, green foliage, faster than a flash of lighting. The poacher stared the gorilla directly in the eyes. It was a challenge. The Silverback tackled him to the ground. He turned for the second man, who screamed loudly. The massive beast took this as a challenge and tackled the second man. His next screams were screams of agony. The third man tried to run away. The Silverback whipped around and with a tremendous roar and beating of his chest, grabbed the man and tossed him like a rag doll, having the strength of eight men.

They froze in place. Kevin told everyone to not run or scream, and to be extremely quiet and lower their eyes. He and Dr. Fred both made a humming, rumbling sound deep in their chests.

"Hmm …" And again, "hmm." Both men took turns making the deep, rumbling sound. It was working; the Silverback was calming down from his rage. On all fours, walking on his knuckles, the nearly 600-pound, powerfully built gorilla calmly strolled up to Ebony to retrieve his twin sons.

Ebony shut her eyes tightly and held her breath as the gorilla approached her. No one moved. He took the first baby, and the second climbed onto his father. He cradled them gently, then with a grunt, he turned and walked back into the forest, his twin boys clinging to his black fur. In shocked silence, they all stood for several minutes, not saying a word. Only the moans of the three injured poachers could be heard.

"That was *awesome!*" Storm shrieked, adjusting her hat as it nearly tumbled off the top of her head. "Cherie, did you see that? That was *awesome!*" she repeated again, hugging Cherie.

"Oh my gosh, oh my gosh, oh my gosh!" Yalani mumbled over and over, still in a bit of shock. Her guide Jimbo fanned her face with a giant palm leaf.

"Valerie?" Cherie asked, "Please tell me you got that on video?"

She nodded yes, the camera's video still recording.

* * *

"Ebony? Ebony?" Cherie touched her gently on the shoulder and called her again.

Ebony stood her eyes still tightly shut. "Wait, wait, wait," she stammered, holding out her empty arms. She opened one eye and looked around, afraid the gorilla might still be there. Cherie took a hold of her outstretched hands, calming her. She fell into Cherie's arms, weakened from the fright. She stood there for several minutes longer, just holding on and trying to feel safe again.

Cherie allowed her to calm herself and asked, "Ebony, are you okay?" Her face was buried against Cherie's shoulder, and she mumbled incoherently. "I'm sorry, I couldn't understand what you said. Are you okay?"

Lifting her head from Cherie's shoulder, she nodded, yes and spoke. This time more clearly. "Like, oh my god, like he *stank* so bad!"

They all burst into laughter.

EPILOGUE

After a night of celebrating at camp, the girls wearily climbed into bed and slept. The next morning, they packed and were ready to go. Of course, Storm had to eat one more bowl of *katogo* before the long trip back to Kampala.

They hugged, waved, and said their goodbyes. This had been the best, most exciting trip ever. They'd learned so many new things about the rainforest and about themselves.

They would miss Uganda, their new friend Dr. Fred, and of course they would especially miss Kevin, their guides, and the twin gorilla babies whose lives they'd helped save.

"Kevin," Cherie gave him high praise. "We could not have asked for a better guide. We had a great time. Thank you for keeping us safe. We'll be in contact to check on their progress."

They finished their conversation, said their last tearful goodbyes, and waved as Kevin drove away.

As they walked toward the airline counter, their phones dinged at the same time. "Diva mail, diva mail!" It was an incoming message from Dr. Khambrel back home in San Francisco.

Cherie answered her watch. "Dr. Khambrel! Hello, how are you? We're at the airport getting ready to check-in for our flight back to San Francisco."

"Yes, yes, which is precisely why I'm calling," he said. "Two things. Firstly, I want to again congratulate you and the Divas on a job well done. You did fantastic. I monitored your progress at every step of the way and knew you would complete this mission with great success. I had all faith in you and your team. Which brings me to my second reason for calling." Dr. Khambrel hesitated with the next bit of news and started out by clearing his throat.

"Ahem, well," he said. "I have bad news and devastating news. Which would you like to hear first?"

"Bad news first," Cherie said, bracing for what was coming.

She waved for the girls to come closer. They needed to hear the bad news as well. This would affect them all. She put Dr. K, as the girls called him, on speakerphone.

"You will not be coming back to San Francisco right away," he announced.

They gave a collective moan of disappointment. Although they loved Uganda, the rainforest, Kevin, and especially the twin gorilla babies, they wanted to get back to the academy to sleep in their own beds.

"Oh no, oh my gosh," said Yalani.

"What? Not going home?" said Kyloni.

"What's happening? I didn't hear what he said," said Storm.

"Shh, be quiet and listen!" said Ebony.

Valerie recorded it all.

"This mission, if you choose to accept, will take you 12,648 kilometers away from Uganda to the city of Brisbane Queensland, Australia, where wildfires are burning out of control. Millions of animals are at risk, like kangaroos and koalas." Dr. Khambrel could hardly be heard over their commotion.

"How many miles is that?"

"Did he say Biz Brain?"

"No, silly, he said Brisbane."

"That's 7,859 miles!"

"Shh, quiet down!"

"Ladies," Cherie interrupted. "Are we going to accept this assignment?" she asked.

They all gave a resounding, "*yes!*"

"Well Divas, looks like we have a change in plans. We'll have to rush to catch our flight. It leaves in thirty minutes," she said, checking her watch.

"We're going to Australia, mate! We're going to Australia, mate!" Storm sang as she danced in a circle around the group, tossing poor little Spinderella around in her bug carrier.

They gathered in a circle, each reaching their right hands in the middle, one stacked on top of the other led by Cherie. "Okay, on the count of three," she counted, "One, two, three … Wildlife Divas!"

With that, Storm jumped high in the air and shouted, "We're going to *Australia!*"

Valerie caught the image midjump. It was the perfect boomerang moment.

Off they ran, full speed to catch their flight.

THE END

ACKNOWLEDGMENTS

To Professor Eric Koester of Georgetown University's Creator Institute, thank you for believing in my story idea and for giving me the opportunity to share it with the world. To New Degree Press and Whitney McGruder, my editor, my word count ninja and author whisperer who quieted my panic on many occasions. To John Saunders, author coach extraordinaire, thank you for seeing what I could not. It was through your eyes I gained confidence. Your research abilities are uncanny and amazing. Thank you for helping me stretch and grow out of my comfort zone.

A sleepless night, an Instagram post, and Kevin Byarugaba, owner/operator of Let's Go Gorilla Uganda, made magic happen for The Wildlife Divas Adventure Team. Before meeting

Kevin, all my research for the book was done using Google and YouTube. Facts about Bwindi Impenetrable National Park and the critically endangered Mountain Gorillas were products of my imagination. Never did I think I'd have the opportunity to actually experience the very things written on the pages of this action adventure of this global educational children's book. To the Let's Go Gorilla Uganda Safari Team, Emmanuel Akankwasa, and Bright Bainomugisha, from the bottom of my heart, a thunderous hand clapping applause and thank you for the most extraordinary safari.

To Doris Gaines, my friend and travel adventurer, thank you for *living out loud* with me, bearing witness to all the trials, tribulations, and successes.

To Doctor Fred Nizeyimana, Field Veterinarian with the Gorilla Doctors of the University of California Davis, an ally and supporter of this children's book that brings attention to the plight of these magnificent creatures, I thank you most graciously for your knowledge and expertise.

To Mr. Stephen S. Masaba, Director of Tourism and Business Development of the

Ugandan Wildlife Authority. Meeting with you was one of many highlights of the trip. The future seems filled with promise and possibilities.

To my serendipitous meetings, aka, my earth angels. To the incredible people I've met during my travels who have had such positive impacts on my life. In Peru, Sofia Ruzo, my talented illustrator, whom I met dressed as *Game of Thrones*' very own Daenerys Targaryen. In Dubai, Isaias Medina III, you are my superhero plain and simple! Desmond Chu, I am forever grateful for your help. And here in my own home state of California, Sharon A. Fox and LaLa the Lamb of the Princess Channel, what a delight it has been meeting you.

A thunderous uproar of applause and thanks to my hometown folks of Richmond Heights, Miami, Florida, my Northern California family, close friends, and all those who supported me via social media with thoughts, comments, well wishes, and prayers for my success. And especially to my contributors and supporters of my Indiegogo Campaign, please accept my most gracious thank you to: Kenya Arledge, Joseph Brown, Aubrey Jackson, Amnoni Meyers, Alex

Anderson, Iolani Bullock, Sam Landon-Jones, Carol Yee, Robert Caveney, Dianne Mills, Prof. Eric Koester, Caitlyn Lubas, Acasia Olson, Alan Hammond, Rosalyn Hunter Berry, Sharon A. Fox, Diane Thompson, Danny Johnson, Lola R. Thomas, Sandra Goldson, Judith Goldson, Gary Callahan, Vivian Price, Doan Winkel, Stephanie Williams, Samuel Reden, Wendell and Brenda Bain, Cynthia Richardson, Joncey Lee, Apryl Armstrong, Daphne Walker, Corina Montes, Amina Samake, Domenique Charles, Cnd Howell, Nic Skidmore, Veronica Rucker, Gwendolyn Johnson, Sam Armstrong, Erica Kidder, Curtis May, Kathy Marshall and last but not least Marty Davis. My cup is eternally filled with gratitude. For your extra added love and support, Sally Casazza, Mimi, Rocky and Yalani Theodore, Hassie Dianne Hill, Shane Rutter, Patricia Cherry, Ebony Gilbert, Kamali Gilbert, Tim and Regina Randolph, Kyloni Randolph, Leslie Randolph, Greg, Annette and Storm Randolph, Eric Randolph Jr., Antwon, Faezeh, and Baran Randolph. And to my Ugandan travel buddy, Doris Gaines. Each and every one of you has had to listen to me drone on endlessly over the years about the Wildlife Divas. I'm sure they are as much a part of your lives as they are mine from having to listen to me talk about them relentlessly. Through my ups and downs, frontward and backward, you have been here for me, and I am grateful to you each and every day. Dreams really do come true. Just believe.